# THE
# SECRET
# SUMMER
# PROMISE

*Keah Brown* ♡

# THE SECRET SUMMER PROMISE

~~~

**KEAH BROWN**

## LQ

**LEVINE QUERIDO**

Montclair | Amsterdam | Hoboken

This is an Arthur A. Levine book
Published by Levine Querido

www.levinequerido.com • info@levinequerido.com

Levine Querido is distributed by Chronicle Books, LLC

Library of Congress Control Number: 2022945155

ISBN 978-1-64614-173-9

Printed and bound in China

Published in May 2023

First Printing

To my cousin, Mykele, the first of us to live out loud, thank you. And to my fellow hopeless romantics, may a love like this happen for us someday, too.

"We are *not* skinny-dipping at the lake house," I said, crossing my arms with a shake of my head.

Hailee huffed, and I smiled, convinced I'd won. I sat back in the uncomfortable stool at Michelle's Ice Cream Shop where we worked, the sun shining through the glass window to the side of us. My best friend and I were the only ones here, on a surprisingly slow afternoon, considering today was the last day of school. We'd had to rush here for our shift, but for now, the shop was empty enough for us to plan.

Excited about my little victory, I fixed Hailee with my most apologetic smile and was already devising what we might do instead this summer. But a challenging smirk of her own stole across Hailee's face.

"Oh, my sweet summer child," Hailee said, "but we are. Did you forget? You used your remaining veto for the year on camping last weekend." I sat up straighter. The sunlight cutting through the window started framing her smile.

I needed to refocus.

"I hate camping. Why would I want to sleep outside, on the ground, when I have a perfectly good bed at home?" I uncrossed my arms and stood. "I refuse to be another mosquito's meal so you can see the same stars we see on my roof all the time."

"Exactly," Hailee said, smugly. I was set up. She'd set me up to use my last veto! She raised her fist in the air like she was in *The Breakfast Club*. Hailee was so dramatic. I walked over and slapped her on the arm before turning on my heel.

"This friendship is a wash," I announced, sitting back down.

"Love you more," Hailee winked. "This is going to be fun, you'll see. Olivia—"

"Won't be there? Dreams really do come true," I cut in.

"Drea, stop it. Olivia, Fiona, and Charlie are already in."

"And dreams die everyday too," I grumbled. "Fine. But I get control of the music in the car." I had to win something out of this summer list.

"Well, I want to control it on the way back. That's only fair."

I scoffed and folded my arms.

"This is a special circumstance," she said. "Call it."

I pretended not to be too eager. We used to settle our disagreements like this all the time, when we were kids. But we'd decided we were too old for it last year on Hailee's sixteenth birthday.

Hailee pulled a coin out of her back pocket and walked back around the counter to me.

"Heads, because yours is so big," I teased with a wink.

"Great, that leaves tails for me, which is perfect because I have the perfect one," she replied, smacking her own butt for emphasis. Hailee tossed the coin in the air and snatched it. She uncovered her hands and sighed. I'd won, I won! It wasn't that Hailee's music taste was bad, per se—I mostly just liked to tease her—but mine was just . . . better.

"Love the swift justice," I said while Hailee rolled her eyes. I patted her shoulder sympathetically. I spent what felt like an eternity trying to ignore the way her returned smile made my insides melt. Being in love with your best friend is such a cliché, and I know it, but here I am, hopelessly and secretly so.

"What? Do I have something?" She patted her face and I tried my best not to smile again. I needed to clear my head.

A couple weeks ago, when I figured out I was bisexual, my head was in Hailee's lap and time stopped. Hailee, a true bibliophile, thought it would be fun to read a book out loud to me, without telling me anything about it. This was something we liked to do every year as school drew to a close, and we had less homework and more time between end-of-the-year exams.

The chapter started off simple enough, two best friends, sitting on the grass in the park, plotting out the rest of their summer— which sounded exactly like a day we would actually have. It was nice, there were sunflowers (my favorite), and one friend started teasing the other. Hailee loved teasing me. It was good, normal, safe. They met up with other friends later to get food at a local diner. Everything shifted as they were driving down a long road, singing songs at the top of their lungs. One friend looked at the other and pulled off into an overlook to watch the stars. They sat in silence for a few moments, then the girl started describing the silkiness of her friend's ink-black hair and the way the passing car lights lit up her face. The other went into detail about all the things she loved about her friend: her bright smile, her big, beautiful eyes, her soft skin, her perfume, and her loud laughter.

Hailee had taken a second to laugh at the cheesiness of the description. Her own laughter boomed through my room. My breath caught in my throat as Hailee continued reading. One character confessed her feelings shakily, quietly, before leaning in slowly. It was then that the truth hit me like a truck. At that moment, the idea of describing and then kissing Hailee in the same way didn't feel so funny as it was exciting, and lying there with her, our faces inches away, the street quiet, I found myself desperate to try it. As Hailee finished the chapter, she laughed once more, softly, and smiled down at me. But my heart was beating too loudly and too fast to really focus on anything. Hailee didn't take her eyes off of me, and I was convinced she could tell, so I pretended my legs hurt and needed to sleep it off. Hailee shrugged and lay down too, shutting off the lights as she went. I didn't sleep at all that night.

"No, you're good, Hail," I sputtered, jolting back out of the memory and into the ice cream shop. The truth is, despite my wildest hopes, I could never do what that character did: I could never tell Hailee about the feelings bubbling up in me. I could not compliment her inky black hair, or reveal the way my heart leapt every time she said my name. I couldn't tell her how cute she looked with flour on her nose after a day spent learning how to bake with my dad, or the way that lately, every time she grabbed my hand, I never wanted her to let go. Telling her would ruin our friendship, because Hailee does not and will never see me that way. I'm not the kind of girl people fall in love with; I'm the girl they look at with pity because I can't spend the summer going to Meena Singh's pool parties, because I had to recover from a surgery. I'm the kind of girl that someone wants kudos for taking to prom, not the person they really want to be there with. I'm the kind of girl who is ready to avoid the inevitable rejection and not let in even the slightest sliver of risk of ruining our friendship. I'm the girl happy to be her best friend for the rest of my life. That will have to be enough.

"Okay, because you were staring."

Hailee adjusted her position from where she now sat next to me behind the counter. Our first set of customers came in a couple minutes later, and we began to divide and conquer. I took the two asking for scoops of rocky road and butter pecan ice cream in bowls, while Hailee took the two who wanted chocolate and vanilla swirls in a cone. The rush picked up as they were leaving, so we put the rest of our discussion aside and kept ourselves busy.

"We're going back to your place, right?" Hailee asked once the last chair was upside-down on a table. I nodded and we headed out to her car. A carefully selected playlist of our favorite songs and the thrill of summer got us to my house in no time. When we arrived, it was empty, so we went straight upstairs to my room. Lying on my bed, Hailee pulled out her phone. I watched as she responded to a few posts and texted her mom back. "You ready?" she asked when she was done. I pulled out my own phone and nodded.

"Let's do this. Best summer ever," I said, opening the Notes app on my phone. Hailee began listing the previously decided items. I felt the familiar rush from planning adventures and was grateful to my brain for giving me a break.

"Actually, can I change out of this uniform? I'll be right back," Hailee said, dashing to the bathroom. I understood not wanting to be reminded of work once it was over, so I decided to change too. We hadn't planned it, but we threw on the same concert tee. I wore mine tied to the side, over a white dress with sunflowers on it, and Hailee wore hers with distressed jean shorts.

"Great minds," I murmured appreciatively. Hailee took a bow, and we both laughed. I heard the door downstairs open and close and I figured it was my dad. He usually got home first.

"I'd expect nothing less from soulmates," Hailee replied easily, and I tried to ignore the way my breath hitched at the idea. None the wiser, she continued on. "As previously discussed, some of these are just for the two of us. Except the skinny-dipping and the amusement park, of course. The girls are already aware." Hailee was talking now in her most authoritative voice. I laughed behind my hand as she glared at me.

"Sorry, your serious voice is funny, but I am focused now," I reassured her.

"Good," Hailee said with a curt nod. I caught the small smile at the edge of her lips.

"We do every item together unless one of us is unable," I added. "In that event, we reconvene and come up with something else." I doubted we would have to worry about being unable to do any of the items on the list though. Hailee and I were the kind of annoying friends who never fought. Olivia, Fiona, and Charlie often joked that we were one vote in activity decisions because we would always agree. This summer wouldn't be any different.

"So, we still have six empty spots to fill," Hailee said, tucking a piece of hair behind her ear. When her tongue poked out to touch her lip, I knew she was seriously thinking about her answers. I had decided mine last night before she'd driven us to school in the morning.

"Three each. My three are: going to the art show two towns over, the Lizzo concert, and sneaking into that 'eighteen and over' night at Blueberries," I announced, putting my phone down and making eye contact.

"Why? We'll never get in. What's the point?" Hailee cried, even though I knew she was going to agree anyway, because this was my skinny-dipping.

"Add it," I said, fixing her with my own curt nod.

"Fine. Added. My three are: going to that new paintball place that just opened, the pop-up thrift shop, and a Drew Barrymore movie marathon," Hailee said.

"Boring, but sure." I stood up and walked over to my bed to sit next to her. She scooted over and waited for me to settle in place.

"Hey! You love Drew. And every item can't be skinny-dipping. Which, by the way, was my idea!"

"I know," I teased.

"Just making sure!" Hailee assured, pressing her free hand to her chest like she was frightened by the idea that I may have forgotten.

"Are we posting?" I asked, though I already knew the answer. Yes, we post because we're teenagers who enjoy social media. And though combing through your own feed to try and figure out if your best friend is in love with you isn't *the* healthiest of ways to decide when—or if—to tell her, I had run out of options.

"Of course we are, we love content. And maybe, there will be moments we don't want to forget," Hailee laughed. Stomach meets somersaults.

I put my phone facedown on my bed and cleared my throat, desperate to get back on track. I'd never used to be this nervous around my best friend. I'd never had a reason to be, but now, everything felt different. In an effort to keep busy, I cuffed one sleeve of my shirt.

"Here, let me help you." Hailee turned toward me and cuffed my left sleeve. "There, perfect."

"Girls! Cookies. Get them while they're hot!" my dad interrupted, calling up the stairs. Phew. Hailee jumped up and ran to the door. She turned at the last moment, smiling at me. I fought a sudden urge to tell her right then and there.

"I love the-first-day-of-summer cookies. See you down there?" She yelled excitedly back to my dad: "Coming!" I breathed easier as she stepped out of the room.

Scrolling through my phone, I closed out the open apps and went back to the list. The definitive list of things to make this summer the best one yet. The list that was supposed to make me the best version of myself. The list looked back at me, the both of us brimming with possibility.

**THE BSE (Best Summer Ever) LIST!**

1. Blueberries
2. Art show in ShoeHorn
3. Lizzo concert
4. thrift shop pop-up
5. Skinny-dipping at the lake house
6. Amusement Park Day!
7. Drew Barrymarathon
8. Paintball Day

"We can do this," I said out loud to the empty room. This was going to be the best summer ever; I deserved it. I'd been through too much, and I didn't want to second-guess myself anymore. The truth was: I didn't know if I could actually do everything on the list.

But I would try.

This summer, I was going to make my own adventures and memories. This summer was going to be better than every summer before it. In my seventeen years on earth, I had spent too long waiting. Waiting for adventure and thrills to come to me. I was ready for my life to start.

Right now, though, I was exhausted. To be fair, I am almost always tired in some way, because having cerebral palsy means I tire faster than most of the people in my life. Last summer I spent all my time in bed. My most recent surgery took longer to recover from than I had hoped. So, while I was sick and shut in, the girls made sure to check on me. Hailee went the extra mile as she always did. She came over with her never-ending energy, and we marathoned my favorite movies and TV shows. By the time I was up and back at it, school was starting again. My whole summer wasted, spent nursing wounds out of my control.

I stood up, ready to head downstairs to join everyone, but then spotted my easel and the freshly dried painting I had made of my mother and father. It was of them laughing together on the couch. I was probably a sap for thinking so, but the way my parents loved each other was my favorite.

I turned away from the painting and scrolled through social media again, liking posts and laughing at memes. "FIRST DAY OF SUMMER!!" I posted and closed the app. I thought back to my parents, how they'd met when they were in their twenties and my dad knew my mom was the one. I wanted a love like theirs: a love that lasts, a love that wasn't one-sided. Even if I couldn't be honest with Hailee right now, I could stand to be honest with myself. I reopened the list and started typing.

### THE BSE (Best Summer Ever) LIST!

1. Blueberries
2. Art show in ShoeHorn
3. Lizzo concert
4. thrift shop pop-up
5. Skinny-dipping at the lake house
6. Amusement Park Day!
7. Drew Barrymarathon
8. Paintball Day
9. **FALL IN LOVE?**

My phone chimed. A text from Hailee.

Hails: Get down here before I eat all the cookies!

I rolled my eyes and smiled.

Andrea: I'm coming! Cookie Monster!

I opened the picture Hailee attached of herself gazing lovingly at the cookie and groaned. This was going to be harder than I thought.

"Finally!" Hailee announced when I came into her view. I walked behind her and toward my dad, who was by the fridge.

"Hey Daddy," I said, hugging him tightly.

"Aht aht," my dad cut in with a fake stern finger-wag, as I walked back over to Hailee.

"Sorry . . . Hey Baker and Super Dad," I deadpanned, turning to make sure she was hearing him too.

"Is he serious?" she asked.

"Yes, that's really how he refers to himself. He started last week," I said, joining Hailee in laughter we didn't need to hide. My dad, to his credit, was too proud of his new moniker to do anything but bask, like he'd just won an Oscar.

"Hey sweetheart. What were you doing up there?" he asked, leaning his weight against the counter.

"Resting. Where's Mommy?"

I popped a cookie in my mouth and smiled. My dad's baked goods always did have a calming effect on me—kinda like my art. On the baking tray were chocolate chip cookies with peanut butter chunks. I finished the cookie and smiled with my teeth, watching Hailee reach for another.

"Last one before dinner, Hails," Dad said, chuckling at her resulting pout. I laughed too.

"Fine. But I would just like everyone to note my great sacrifice." She really should look into acting. Dad and I played along anyway, praising her for her restraint.

"Noted," I smirked.

"And what a sacrifice it is," Dad added.

"Mom is at the store getting stuff for family dinner," Dad continued, stealing one of his cookies and leaning against the counter again, satisfied. The cooking trait, or gene—whichever you call it—skipped me, but I knew what it was like to take pride in your work. That feeling came through tenfold when other people liked it too. I guess Hailee's obsession with his cookies was a lot like the rush Mom got at fashion shows when people loved her designs, or when four tables sent back compliments to Dad after tasting his signature dish at the restaurant.

"Oh, that reminds me," Hailee said. "My mom asked if you want her to make her world-famous turnovers? She said since you bake for a living, you'd want to take a day off?"

"Hailee, I love Janice, we all do . . . but her turnovers are . . ." Dad trailed off. We shared a look of slight panic.

"Terrible. I know. I told her you wanted to make cheese-cakes because baking for family relaxes you." Hailee smiled at her own quick thinking and tapped the counter.

"Nice save," I said, bumping her shoulder. I got up to stretch, unclenching my fists, before bending to my left side for a hold of fifteen and then to the right for fifteen. Daddy and Hailee joined me for the front-toe touch, counting out loud. When we finished, we sat back around the island. I knew they didn't need to do it with me, but I felt better when they decided to.

"Was my save nice enough for another cookie?" Hailee asked, eyeing the plate in front of her.

"Nope. Go watch TV or something until I call you two for dinner. And don't erase my episodes of *House Hunters* either. I know where you live." The gruffness in Dad's voice let us know he was trying to sound serious, but the twinkle in his eye and the slight smile at the corner of his mouth gave him away, and he blew us each a kiss before shooing us away from the kitchen.

The next morning, I woke up in a panic. I'd been doing so for the past three weeks.

The dreams always started with me being surrounded by the people I love, which made me feel safe and warm. I always got too comfortable, though, under my mom's praise, my dad's laughter, Fiona and Charlie's support, Freddie P and Uncle D's teasing, Faye and Vanessa's excitement, Olivia's forgiveness, Hailee's love . . . all of it making me let my guard down. This was obviously a mistake, because every person then disappeared in front of me, the moment I reach for them. The dream always ended with me cold, alone, and in the dark somewhere.

I involuntarily shivered at the memory. Looking to the right, I found my calendar and took a deep breath. Wednesday,

June 4. After taking another steadying breath, I reached my left hand up to touch the top of my head. At least my sleep cap stayed on last night. Wiping the drool from my mouth, because I am who I am, I got out of bed, stretched, and headed toward my door. The closer I got to the door, the louder the gospel music got. I sang my way down the stairs and through the foyer. When I got to the kitchen, I knew something was up.

"Good morning, baby girl. How are you feeling?" Dad asked, turning off the stove and plating a scrambled-egg, cheese, and sausage sandwich. He put the dish and a glass of orange juice in front of me, smiling apologetically.

"Well, you made my breakfast today, so how worried should I be?" I asked, eyeing the food suspiciously. I took a bite anyway and relished in how great my dad was at making breakfast. "I can taste the hot sauce too. How bad is it?"

The first time my dad made me a full breakfast—unprompted, with my favorites—was when I was really into ceramics. He'd broken the piece I'd worked on for two weeks every day by pulling his car too far into the garage. I was devastated, and gave up ceramics shortly after. Painting came into the picture weeks later, so I got over it, but Dad also got used to the new delivery of bad news.

"Don't be mad, but I have to go into work tonight to do some early recipe testing, because . . . Mom and I have to fly to New York Sunday for a few days, to handle what Fredrick is calling a 'fashion crisis,'" Dad finished, peering over at me with the best "I'm sorry" face that he could muster.

"Which means, no Sunday dinner and no gallery night?" I asked, but already knew the answer.

"There will be other Sundays, and you can still go to the gallery pop-up. We just can't go with you. Fredrick said, 'All hands on deck.' It does sound kinda bad." Dad walked around the counter and hugged me. I was genuinely upset, because I looked forward to our tradition of going to the pop-up every year. But that didn't mean I couldn't milk this for what it was worth, right?

"But it's tradition," I protested. "Pop-up and pizza. Just the three of us. Mom even leaves her phone at home and everything. Are you two skipping out on family time with your not-so-little-girl-anymore? Wow," I pouted. Sure, I'm seventeen, but I love my parents. There wasn't much need for rebellion when you had parents as cool as mine. They never needed to know that, though.

"We're so sorry, sweetie," Mom said, walking into the room and around the counter to hug me from the other side. Evelyn Williams, former-model-turned-fashion designer, and mom. My mom. I was very lucky. She was still the most gorgeous person in every room. I sat up straighter as she walked toward me. I loved the sound of her heels as she moved. Squeezing me once, she turned toward my dad.

With my mom here, though, I couldn't milk this abandonment the way I'd hoped.

"How long were you standing there waiting to bring me the bad news?" I asked. I looked over at her, arm still around

Dad's waist. Mom looked super guilty. I tried my best not to smile. I was so getting a bonus gift out of this still. Maybe not as many as I wanted, but at least two.

"Long enough to figure out how to make it up to you. Dinner, just the two of us?" Mom offered. I smiled with my mouth closed, eyes big, emoting the appropriate amount of disappointment. My performance was about to win an Oscar.

"I'm listening. But what about New York?" I asked. I knew the extra ask was risky, but all great artists take risks. Here I was, waiting as the host praised my fellow nominees. In this fantasy, Hailee was squeezing my hand, and I was trying and failing not to get my hopes up.

"We'll bring you back new paints?" Dad suggested, looking at Mom to confirm. Mom nodded quickly, then looked back at me. I could tell she was on to me now, but she said nothing, fixing me with her famous, "I'll-allow-this-only-once" sly smile.

"Now you're talking. Throw in that new jumpsuit from the upcoming fall line I saw last week, and we're even," I said, leaping up from my seat. All traces of sadness were gone. I mentally accepted my award and thanked the guilt coursing through my parents' veins.

"Did she just swindle us, D?" Mom laughed, watching me pull out my phone and start texting.

"I believe so, E. I believe so." Dad shook his head and started cooking breakfast for them.

"I'll be in my room if you need me," I finished, waving to my parents and walking out of the room.

"Pleasure doing business with you, Drea," Mom called out with a laugh.

"The pleasure was mine!"

When I got to my room, I shut the door behind me and did a happy dance. I would miss my parents, for sure, but new paints and that cute jumpsuit were a real win. At least I would start the new school year in style. I paired my phone to the speakers on my dresser. Sabrina Carpenter came up on shuffle first, Jessie J after, and Beyoncé and Kehlani after that.

As I danced around my room, cleaning before dinner, I caught a glimpse of a picture from the past, one with just me and Olivia. My mind wandered. Back to when I was a kid, and Olivia and I were real best friends—not just tolerating each other to spare our other best friends. We used to have dance parties in Olivia's room while Annie, Olivia's nanny, made us lunch. Just before the picture in question was taken, Olivia had made me promise not to leave her like her parents so often did. I didn't know when I made the promise, that she would be the first to leave.

"No need to dwell on the past. That was a long time ago," I said to no one. I was a little tired from the dancing, so I stopped and paused the music as I finished cleaning. Sitting in my chair to give my aching calves a rest, I pulled out my phone and played a match-three game until dinner. We had Dad's "special" mac and cheese. It was delicious.

"Hails, you can't just say that someone is in a TV show when they're not," I said as a new round of customers walked into the shop. I smiled at them and made their two banana splits while Hailee made their root beer float. After they left, satisfied, Hailee picked the conversation back up.

"Jaime Pressly is in *Hart of Dixie*," Hailee stated, definitively. I looked over at her, her hair slightly curled and pulled back from her face. Summer had just begun, but it was already so hot that I'd spent the last thirty minutes periodically wiping sweat from my forehead while she sat next to me, gorgeous and very wrong.

"King. Jaime King is in *Hart of Dixie*," I said, laughing as she rolled her eyes.

"Stand up, I need your phone," Hailee said. I did as I was told. I held my breath as Hailee slipped it out of my back pocket, grateful she was none the wiser. I had no idea where her phone was, or why she hadn't gone to get it, but I wasn't going to complain.

"See!" Hailee exclaimed, pushing the screen directly in front of my eyes, then looking at it herself.

"Yeah, I do, and just as I said . . ." I laughed again. Hailee pulled the phone back to her face, her mouth falling open in surprise. "Now what do I get for being right?" I asked, raising my eyebrow.

"What do you want?" Hailee replied, her face serious as she bit her lip.

"I-I—" My mouth went dry. And then the bell on the door dinged. Five teenage boys from our school's soccer team walked in. Liam Mitchell was in front, and the first to reach the counter.

"Hey ladies, how's it hanging?" Liam asked.

"We're good, what can we get you?" Hailee said, pulling out a pen and paper.

"Well since your number isn't on the menu . . ." Liam trailed off, winking at Hailee.

"It's not," Hailee replied, but I didn't miss the smile playing on her lips. Wait . . . did she like Liam? He'd spent the last half of the year hitting on her, and she'd seemed disinterested, but now . . . maybe less so?

Was Liam the type of person Hailee could see herself with? Was he going to be the one to make her laugh or smile?

Was he the person who would be her high school sweetheart, who she'd walk down the aisle to, a little after college graduation, while I stood off to the side, silently holding the pieces of my broken heart in my hands?

Hailee cleared her throat, pulling me from my nightmare. Sure, it was a bit dramatic, but as we have already established, I can be.

"Well, in that case, I'll take two scoops of Oreo ice cream," Liam smiled. "I love a Thursday special." He turned and winked at me.

"Hey, it's nice to see you both," a brown-haired boy with green eyes said, stepping up to the counter. George Fallon, the most popular boy in our grade more specifically. But he didn't even glance Hailee's way. I looked behind me to see if there was someone else there, then pointed to myself. "Yeah, you," he laughed, running a hand through his hair. The others placed their orders and stepped to the side, but George sat at the stool in front of me and just chilled. Hailee and I made quick eye contact as she started on their orders.

"Do you know what you want?" I asked as he smiled at me again.

"What's your favorite?" he replied, leaning in like he was hearing vital information.

"I like the butter pecan," I said easily. If it were anyone else, I'd have assumed they were flirting, at least a little. But the most popular boy in school? He had me confused with someone else.

"Noted, I'll take three scoops in a bowl," George said with a wink. Winking was a team quirk, apparently. I stepped to the side to start scooping his ice cream while he paid with Hailee. When I handed it to him, he purposefully made our fingers touch. He bit his lip and laughed a little. Hailee cleared her throat, her slight annoyance clear only to me.

"Come on G, we gotta go," Liam called out.

"Hope to see you around," George said, walking backward toward the door.

"You do?" I asked incredulously.

"I do," he said, with one last smile, and then he was gone.

"What was that?" Hailee asked as the door and its bell rang shut. She looked at me skeptically, her hand on her hip, pushing her apron forward a little. She cleared her throat while waiting for my response.

"I have no idea!" I promised, though I found myself looking anywhere but at her, tapping my fingers on the counter, and letting a few pieces of hair fall to the side of my face. The rest of our shift went by without much excitement. We didn't talk anymore about the boys.

~~~~~

When I got into Hailee's car after we finished, she decided that she wasn't ready to go home, and texted her mom for permission to get a car wash. Even though I was the only person in our friend group that couldn't drive, I loved car washes. We pulled up to Sud's and got in line. The day was still hot and sticky—the wind had found someplace else to keep cool. Since we'd opened at the shop that morning, we were done by three, and we now had two-and-a-half hours before dinner. Anything felt possible.

Hailee lined the car up with the track and put it in neutral. She flexed her hands on the steering wheel, looking forward. Then she started tapping to the beat of the song. Finally, she faced me.

"How weird was it that George was flirting with you?"

"He wasn't flirting with me," I said. "*Liam* was flirting with you! George probably thought I was someone else." I gave her a quick look and then turned up the radio. We sang along to a few songs at the top of our lungs until the wash was over. But then, Hailee turned the volume back down.

"Liam flirts with everyone, and who would George confuse you with?" she asked, rolling her window down to tip the guys wiping the car down. She wasn't letting this go.

"I don't know."

"You seemed to be enjoying his attention," Hailee started, and her voice wavered accusingly as she chewed her lip. She kept her eyes on the empty parking lot in front of us as I kept my eyes on her, until she looked at me. She let her lip go and closed her eyes briefly. Something she only did when she was trying to clear her head. She tried to smile, but it came out like more of a wince. I wanted to know what was up in that head of hers that she needed to clear so bad, but she'd tell me eventually. We put the windows down and the sun shone on me. I let out a contented sigh, my arm flying out of the window of its own accord.

Still, I couldn't help myself: "What is that supposed to mean?"

"Nothing," Hailee replied quietly. She pulled out of the parking lot and onto the road again. Then she turned the radio back up, signaling the end to that conversation. Honestly, I didn't mind.

"Want to go to Theresa's Antiques?" I asked, eager to prolong being outside. Hailee loved Theresa's; she dragged us there as often as she could.

"They're closed today," Hailee said. "I think Theresa said she was going to scout for more treasures. Let's go to your favorite place, I'm starving."

When we pulled up to our local grocery store, Dashers, I didn't hide the widening smile on my face. It really was my favorite place; there was just something about being around a lot of food that comforted me. We looped around the tall, tan building with its red roof a few times, trying to find a spot. I had forgotten my accessible parking placard in my mom's car, but even the long walk could not steal my joy. As we walked inside, I said hi to Brian and Owen, the security guards.

"Hey you two, there's a new chicken finger sub over at the bistro that you're going to love," Owen said. He was a tall, older white man in his early fifties with a surprisingly full head of gray hair. Brian, his twenty-something son, was his spitting image—except he had a few less wrinkles and a full head of black hair. As far as facial features, though, it was as if Brian had stolen his dad's entire face.

"Really? I can't wait. Come on, Hails," I squealed, placing my hand in hers and pulling her forward. She waved a goodbye for the both of us before we left their line of sight. We made it to the Bistro—the sandwich station inside the supermarket—in record time. Was I lightly jogging, despite the fact it was nowhere near closing time? Maybe. I let go of Hailee's hand and bounced up to the counter. I ordered us two subs, a side of fries to share, and two lemonades, while Hailee found a table. When we sat down and waited for our food, I spoke up.

"Isn't this so nice?" I placed my chin in my hands and sighed dreamily. Looking at the people around us, I grinned. I saw at least five or six people I knew in some way or the other. That was the fun part about people-watching in a town like ours: seeing the folks you sort of knew and imagining what their lives were like.

"You always get so wistful and cheesy when we come here," Hailee teased. She watched the crowd around us too, though, until our order was called. I got up to grab us extra napkins, and by the time I got back, Hailee had everything displayed neatly. Packets of honey mustard and ketchup became our centerpiece.

"Because it's so great, Hails. I don't have finals or homework to worry about. It's the start of summer, and I don't have a worry in the world." Well, secretly being in love with my best friend was one, but that she didn't need to know about. We ate in a comfortable silence before tossing our garbage away and heading back to the car.

"Well, thanks for going on a date with me, Drea," Hailee said, buckling her seat belt and turning up the radio.

"Is that what this was?" I asked, laughing through the small hope bubbling in my chest. We turned back down the street and passed the last standing video store in town.

"I'm joking," Hailee said, turning at the last second into the convenience store two shops over. "I mean, could you imagine?" she laughed. The bubble of hope inside me died a cold, harsh death.

"Um, no. But . . . why are we stopping here?" I took off my seat belt and exited the car faster than I normally would.

"I need chocolate-covered pretzels and a piece of cheesecake," Hailee called over the car. "They're cheaper here."

We walked inside and grabbed the items she was after in relative silence, but my mind wouldn't stop racing. I couldn't burst into tears at her rejection, because she was standing right next to me, and that wasn't going to help anything. So, I bought some Twizzlers and tore the bag open as soon as we got back in the car.

Hailee let out an annoyed huff as she started the car, then turned to me. I didn't let my heart race as she looked at me like I'd run over her foot with a shopping cart.

"Give me your hands. Both of them," she demanded, her eyes determined, her hands out to me, palms up.

"Why?" I raised an eyebrow and kept my hands firmly in my lap. Hailee scoffed, rotating her wrists impatiently.

"No questions. Give them," Hailee repeated, her frustration now set in her eyebrows, her mouth a thin line. I sighed and gave her my hands. She held them for a moment, then let them go, tucking her hair behind each ear and searching my face, tilting her head from left to right, her tongue poked out a little in concentration. Like it was whenever she studied my art. Whatever she found made her features soften. She took my hands once more.

"You never open a bag that fast unless you're upset, but we just left your favorite place . . . so what happened between then and now?"

"Nothing, just really wanted one, that's all," I replied, with a smile. Though it was clear from the skeptical look creasing her annoyingly cute, freckled face that she didn't believe me.

"Was it Liam? Or the date comment?" Hailee pressed, her voice softer now. Liam, with his curly, brown, shoulder-length hair and deep, hazel eyes. When he smiled, I saw the appeal; I'd melt a little too. I didn't need the reminder that there was always going to be some guy ready and willing to give Hailee the love I'd never be allowed to.

"Drea, I'm sorry about the date joke. I didn't mean to make you think you were undateable or anything. The question surprised me is all and I—"

"Hails, breathe. It's fine," I promised. Hailee's eyes fell away from me and to her lap.

"But it's not fine, not if I hurt you. It's not like I meant that no one would ever date you. Of course they would. You're funny, gorgeous, talented and—" Hailee's mouth and mind were moving a mile a minute; I knew because of the crinkle line on her forehead, still visible though she was no longer looking my way.

"I'm fine, Hailee. Okay?" I finished, watching as she evened out her breathing and looked back up at me.

"Okay," she whispered, squeezing my hands once before letting them go. We put on our seat belts and pulled out onto the road. I turned up the radio and let the music clear my mind.

We sang the way that we always did, the summer sun our spotlight, the passing cars our stage. I would miss this the most if I gave Hailee the chance to reject me: belting out songs in her mom's car, the day ahead of us, tomorrow feeling more full of promise than it ever had. I'd miss the way she looked over at me during red lights, the chorus swelling, my heart racing in time with the beat and the urge to lay down the strands of her hair flying free, as she sang loudly and on-key, offsetting my horrible voice.

Hailee dropped me off at home shortly after and I spent the rest of the afternoon sitting on my back patio, switching between reading and soaking in the sun. Mom and Dad joined me now and again, then we ate dinner on the patio. As night fell, before I could try and stop it, the pesky mosquitoes came with it and I rushed inside, but still ended up with a few bites on my back. Sleep came to me too many hours later, Hailee's "Can you imagine?" laughter replaying in my mind.

I woke up to Hilary Duff. My alarm for the next two weeks was set to one of her songs: "Breathe In. Breathe Out." Fredrick, my mom's best friend and right hand at work, chose it for me. I chose "Please Don't Fall in Love" by VINCINT for them. Every two weeks we picked songs for each other's alarms as a way to stay in touch between visits.

I turned the alarm off to find a slew of text messages. The usual good mornings from my group chats with the girls and Faye and Vanessa. I responded, and put my phone back on my nightstand. After showering and changing for the day, I slipped my phone into my back pocket and headed downstairs. My parents had already left for work, so I was spending a gloriously warm summer Friday alone.

I would probably text the girls to see what they were up to later, but right now, I was excited to see what I could get into by myself. I could order a pizza and eat all of it alone, but it was 11 a.m. so maybe that was just a touch too early. I could paint all day, but I didn't want to necessarily stay in the house the whole time. I walked over to the fridge to grab a snack and there it was, staring right at me: my plan. A black-and-white flyer with flowers all along its border, held up by a magnet of the New York City skyline.

It read:

*Come Shake Your Groove Thang with Groove*
    *Ground at Oak Park!*
*Time: 1:15 p.m. to 3:15 p.m.*
*Admission: Free!!*

I ran back upstairs to change out of the lilac-colored, flowy dress I had on and into a pair of Bermuda jean shorts and a *Never Been Kissed* poster T-shirt. Hailee was right: I really did love Drew Barrymore. I snagged a picnic blanket, a little pillow to lean up against the tree that I was going to need to use for back support, and the large tote bag out of my closet, then walked back downstairs, grabbing the ingredients out of the fridge to make lunch and some snacks to take with me. After assembling sandwiches worthy of a few Instagram pictures, I snapped a selfie and sent it to my parents. One of their rules since I'd begun going places alone was to never leave without them seeing the outfit I had on, just in case of emergency. Nothing ever happened of course—but also, if enough people didn't see your cute outfit, did you wear one anyway? I didn't want to take that chance.

The ride to the park was relatively smooth. Lonnie, my Uber driver, laughed at a few of my jokes and dropped me off as close as possible to where the live band was performing. Groove Ground was playing "Sweet Caroline" as I maneuvered around the growing crowd in front of their makeshift stage, then found the perfect tree nearby: in the shade and unoccupied. I set my tote bag down, pulling out the picnic blanket and laying it flat on the ground before positioning the pillow where I needed it to be. I sat down and smiled at a few of the passersby—families and a few people by themselves, just happy to be outside like me. I was reaching for my second sandwich and the can of tea when my phone buzzed in my pocket.

Hails: Where are you and why is it not at your house?

Andrea: The park. There's a live band so I thought I would spend the day chilling here. Why?

Hails: Mom and I are going to the movies. We came by to see if you might want to come?

Andrea: Aw! I love you both but nah. I'm going to stay here a bit longer.

Hails: Okay, love you. See you tomorrow <3
Andrea: See you tomorrow!

After I finished my second sandwich and listened to Groove Ground's last few songs—covers of Stevie Wonder and Whitney Houston—I packed up my bag and called another cab. I made it over to the entrance with minutes to spare. The cab driver was a woman named Helena. She wasn't much of a talker, but was kind enough to tell me how she achieved the perfect crown braid in her dark brown hair. I took notes.

The next day, after lunch, Mom and Dad sat me down again. This time with good news.

"Daddy and I invited the girls to family dinner tonight. We're doing burgers and fries. Dad doesn't feel like cooking tonight," Mom said. Dad playfully rolled his eyes from where he sat. Their flight to New York tomorrow was in the early morning. If I could cook, I wouldn't want to either. I patted his hand sympathetically to let him know that I knew he was doing his best.

"Good! I'm dying to ask Faye where she got that dress she posted online last week," I said excitedly.

"Faye isn't coming. Vanessa either, actually. Their parents couldn't make the drive today, so I was thinking we could FaceTime them? I miss them myself," Mom added. We really didn't get to see them enough because they lived out of state.

"But Fiona, Charlie, Olivia, and Hailee will be here," Dad said, grabbing all of our plates and loading the dishwasher.

"I'm going to finish packing your dad and I's bags," Mom said, a mischievous gleam in her eyes. "You know if I let him do it, he'd forget everything."

"Hey!" Dad protested. She dodged his swat and ignored him, laughing all the way to their room.

~~~

Hours after watching too many episodes of reality TV, I decided I wanted to change for dinner. When I got upstairs, I switched into a white tank top and jean shorts. There was still some time before the girls got here, so I busied myself playing my favorite match-three game. I'd beaten three levels and was ready for my victory lap with the fourth when my mom called up the stairs.

"Olivia is here!"

I took a deep breath and stood. "Okay, coming!" I called back. Walking down the stairs and through the foyer, I tried to prepare myself for the oncoming awkwardness.

The thing was, Olivia and I were best friends once. Out of our friend group, we had known each other the longest—since we were four. When we fell out after our big blowup in middle school, years earlier, we'd decided to stay "friends" for the sake of the others. But the truth was, we really didn't like each other that much anymore. I know people don't use the phrase frenemy nowadays, but that's what my mom called us. And, it fit the bill. I just wish my mom weren't so sad and wistful when she said it.

Before I could be seen, I stopped by the living room entrance to get a peek of what I was heading into.

"Olivia, how have you been? It's been so long since you've been here," Mom said, sitting on the loveseat across from the couch.

"I've been good, just really busy," Olivia responded, her blond hair and tanned, white skin framed by the sunlight through the window. "The soccer team keeps me pretty occupied. I miss you and Dad W, though."

"Aw! We miss you too. How are your parents doing?" Mom asked.

"Oh, you know. They're even busier than me," Olivia answered, her eyes shifting. It was an open secret that Merv, the family driver, and Olivia's former nanny, Annie, had done more raising of her than her parents had. But Olivia always acted like everything was perfectly fine, even to the people who knew it wasn't.

"It must be nice to have your dad back from sabbatical," Mom smiled, humoring Olivia's lie. She stood. "Want anything to drink, sweetie?"

"Yeah, I'll take a lemonade if you have one? The house looks great by the way."

"Sure thing, and thank you. It really is great to have you back here."

Mom walked into the kitchen, busting me where I stood. She raised one eyebrow, which in almost every Black household meant, "Don't push your luck." I silently huffed but walked into the living room, finally. Olivia Livingston—with her perfectly-made, high blond ponytail, black jeans, pink top, and jean jacket—sat on my couch. Her back was ramrod straight and her head was held high, her legs crossed at the ankles like a princess, as if she had something to prove. Like she hadn't spent most of her childhood in this house.

We didn't say anything, but looked at each other as I walked around the couch and sat down. "Here you go sweetie," Mom announced a few moments later, coming back with the lemonade. "Why don't you two head up to Andrea's room? I'll let the others go up when they get here."

"Thank you, Mama Ev, you really are the best. Lead the way, Andrea," Olivia said, accepting the glass.

Upstairs the silence stretched on. I sat and started scrolling through my phone. I didn't think it was my job to make small talk, and Olivia must've felt the same way, because she wasn't forcing it either. She walked around my room, eyeing the pictures on my wall. Thinking about it, she hadn't been here in years; probably since the time we were still real friends. In the years that had followed, we'd tended to hang at the other girls' houses as a group, steering clear of each other's homes.

"I'm surprised to see myself still here," Olivia said, letting her fingers graze the picture of the two of us as kids. I rolled my eyes.

"Why? You were the one who checked out of our friendship, not me," I replied, looking at my phone.

"You replaced me fast enough," she said, her eyes still scanning the pictures on the wall.

"That was a long time ago. It doesn't matter anymore." I walked over to where Olivia stood. We both stared at the picture for a few more seconds.

"Right," Olivia finished, turning away from the wall and putting some distance between the two of us. "Let's change the subject. I can't believe Hails convinced you to go skinny-dipping. Though, she does seem to be able to convince you easily all the time . . . I wonder why?"

Olivia smirked, her blond ponytail swaying as she crossed her well-toned arms across her chest, perfectly manicured French-tip nails tapping against her chin. Her nose crinkled and her mouth turned up to the left as she pretended to think. I'd forgotten what it was like to be teased by her. For the briefest of moments, I allowed myself to indulge in it while she pointed her "we both know the answer" arched eyebrow at me.

"Shut up. You're doing it too. What convinced you?" I asked. Olivia laughed. She surveyed the rest of the room and settled on the portrait of my parents in the corner.

"I'm not going to look like this forever. I might as well." Olivia crouched down in front of the painting, still half-covered. She glanced back at me and I nodded my head. I watched as she pulled the covering off and gasped loud enough for us both to hear. I felt my walls slam right back up.

"What's wrong with it?" I shot out defensively, walking over to cover the painting back up.

"Nothing. I hate to compliment you, because that's the last thing you need, but Drea . . . this is beautiful."

"Oh," I said.

"Yeah," Olivia said.

"Hey ladies!" Hailee said, walking into my room and cutting the tension. She stopped short and watched us. "Am I interrupting something?" Hailee looked at me and I shrugged. Olivia stood back up and pushed the invisible lint off of her pant leg.

"Absolutely not. I need to use the bathroom," she replied, bustling out of the door before either of us could respond. Hailee walked over to my bed and sat.

"You two are still so awkward around each other," she laughed. I walked over to my curtains. Missing the sun, I opened them and let it slip through and wash over my face. I loved summer so much, and I felt like it loved me back. Even though it wasn't the love I was really after, I would still take it. I closed my eyes, letting the light shine on me.

"Well, you three insist on keeping the both of us around, so . . ." I trailed off, eyes still closed as I took a deep breath.

"Yes, we do. And I'll find a way to make you two actual friends again," Hailee assured.

"I'm sure of it, unfortunately." I opened my eyes and turned back toward Hailee, who challenged me with a raised eyebrow.

"Sure, of what?" Olivia asked, coming back into the room but staying close to the door. I was certain she'd bolt before the night was over anyway. My mom always said I shouldn't be so quick to judge, but if the shoe fits . . .

"A is just being dramatic. Ignore her," Hailee said.

"Ignoring her is fine by me," Olivia replied. She came further into the room and stood across from Hailee, turning her back to me entirely. "Fi and Char are around the corner. Fi's driving."

"So, they'll be here in an hour? Got it," Hailee chuckled. I stood up quickly and walked toward the door. I turned and waited until both Hailee and Olivia's eyes were on me. I watched them for a moment, my best friend, and my former— who liked each other with nary a thought of my feelings in the matter. They were genuine friends still, and I didn't understand how that could be. I couldn't really blame Hailee, though; being nice to everyone was sort of her thing.

"Let's wait for them downstairs, there's not enough room in here for Olivia's ego," I said. Olivia turned around and pushed past me without another word. I ignored her, but found myself transported back to earlier this year in an empty high school hallway. This time, Olivia was standing in front of me, her hands balled up in fists at her side, mirroring my own. "Where do you get off telling anyone about my mother?" I seethed. Who did she think she was? My mom worked very hard to keep her private life private. I wasn't going to let my ex best friend get in the way of that.

"I didn't tell anyone anything they didn't already know. All I did was tell a few stories and said that when I was a kid, she was like a second mother to me, and that she was everything people believed." Olivia rolled her eyes and crossed her arms. "Now, you on the other hand, well, you're just–"

"You're not going to use my mother for clout or popularity," I cut in, taking a step toward her before shifting my weight from my left leg to the right.

"You really are such a hypocrite," Olivia spat. "You preach about the importance of family and friendship, but you immediately assume the worst of me, a person you used to consider as both."

"I'm not doing this with you. Keep my mother's name out of your mouth," I snapped back, turning to walk away.

"So, that's it? You're just going to leave?" Olivia shouted.

I whirled back around to face her. "You taught me how."

Swatting my shoulder, Hailee pulled me back to the room.

"Hello! Drea? Are you even listening to me?" Hailee asked, hand on her hip. She looked like she was seconds from saying: "I'm not angry; I'm disappointed." So, I didn't brush it off.

"Sorry, what?" I asked. The promise Olivia and I had made to the girls was to be at least civil enough to keep the group together. But civility was harder than it looked outside of the school hallways, or when we weren't all together. Having Olivia here alone in my home for the first time in years was bringing up memories I was desperate to bury. We walked downstairs to join the others. At the end of the staircase, Hailee spoke again.

"I said, maybe try talking like a normal human being to Liv—let's not make the entire night awkward, yeah?" Hailee laughed.

"Yeah, okay," I agreed.

"Thank you. I thought I lost you for a second." She wiped a piece of lint off of her shirt and stepped toward me. She smelled like her lavender body wash and the peppermint gum she loved to chew. Hailee was now close enough that I could cradle her face. Best friends didn't cradle each other's faces, so I wouldn't . . . but I could.

I moved to put more space between us. I was not going to spend this night pining. I had to pull it together.

"You're right, you do need to pull it together," Hailee said easily. Doing little to hide the horrified look on my face, I huffed at the ease of her agreement.

"Do you not know you do that thing where you accidentally say part of your thoughts out loud?" Hailee teased.

"No," I said, dropping my head in my hands.

"Don't worry, as your best friend, I can't and won't tell anyone. Plus, it's cute." Hailee squeezed my shoulder and walked past me through the foyer, to the living room. My dad was there, but my mother and Olivia were nowhere to be found. Where did they go? After a moment, I spotted them coming back into the room. My mom had a comforting arm around Olivia, saying something softly to her while they both looked at the ground. What was that about? Their heads snapped up at the same time when they saw me, Mom patted her shoulder one more time before joining Hailee and my dad. Olivia remained where she was standing, so I decided to get it over with.

As I began to walk, I let my armor fall piece by piece beside me. By the time I reached my target, I was confident it wasn't going to be as bad as I'd been steeling myself for. Olivia, who startled easily, jumped when she realized how close I was. As she glared at me, I began to plan my exit, but then I spotted Hailee, who gave me a thumbs up and a smile from where she stood talking with my parents. I hated that smile, because I knew it was going to make me stay and try. Disgusting.

"I just wanted to call a truce. We make this work usually; there's no reason the summer needs to be different," I said quickly. Olivia eyed me and then took a step back, tilting her head toward the foyer where the others would be out of earshot. I followed her into the foyer, where Olivia turned on her heel so fast I almost bumped into her, but I caught myself.

"It won't be awkward," Olivia launched in. "My friends love you for some reason, and yours love me for some reason. They just happen to be the same people. There is nothing we can do about that. Call it a truce if you want to."

"Okay," I agreed. I stood there frozen for a moment until we heard a knock at the door. I opened it to find Fiona and Charlie Perez, our other two best friends, on the other side.

"Am I as old as I feel?" Charlie asked. Fiona hit her arm. I stepped aside so they could enter. Charlie wore her long, black hair in a single, thick French braid, black-and-white Converses, and a T-shirt dress. Fiona shrugged her shoulders. "I ask because Fi took a whole year to get here."

"You're alive, are you not?" Fiona asked, sitting down to take off her strappy, black sandals. Her black cut-off shorts and vintage concert tee complemented her light-brown skin. She stood so Charlie could sit and remove her own shoes.

"Barely," Charlie supplied as I hugged Fiona. Charlie joined us, our arms interlocking at either side of me.

"I didn't scratch you, did I?" I asked. Sometimes my nails grew faster than I could have them cut. It's a whole thing.

"No, you're good," they said in unison. My parents and Olivia said quick hellos and goodbyes as they passed us to go get the burgers and food for everyone. I didn't know why Olivia was going with them. It wasn't like she was going to get extra credit or brownie points by sucking up.

Fiona and Charlie walked over to the kitchen and joined Hailee around the island. I walked over to the couch and turned on the TV. Charlie and Fiona joined me shortly after to figure out what to watch, and Hailee joined us when we landed on a rom-com. I pretended I hadn't seen it and launched into a rehearsed speech about the unrealistic expectations that romantic comedies set. The truth was, though, that I too longed for the same movie-worthy, cheesy love that my friends did. I just knew I shouldn't, because love didn't happen for people like me.

When you watched enough television, read enough books, and saw too many of these movies without seeing yourself in them, you started to get the picture. Don't get me wrong, maybe some Black, disabled, queer people fell in love everyday . . . but I never saw it. What I saw instead were people in soap operas and dramas afraid of becoming disabled like me, or disabled people being sacrificed or killed off in rom-coms and horror movies, or as side characters brought in for a witty line or two and then never seen again. So, while I secretly loved these movies, I knew what was possible for me and what wasn't; I knew I needed to be realistic.

Hailee didn't make it easy—she came and sat right next to me, and I spent the rest of the movie trying and failing to ignore the flutters in my chest every time her leg touched mine or she leaned into me. I may have swooned a little too hard over both the hero and the heroine too, but thankfully, no one seemed to notice.

Everything seemed to have evened out by the time my parents and Olivia returned with the food. Mom called me into the kitchen to help unpack the bags while Olivia and my dad set the table in the dining room. My mom began pulling the burgers and fries out of the bags and setting them on a platter. She moved around me to grab the ketchup and the honey mustard. When she put the napkins on the platter, she spoke up.

"I know it may not seem like it, but everyone is going through something. You're at an age where everything feels weird, exciting, or like, the end of the world," Mom said, as she picked up the platter.

"You have got to stop reading those parenting books." I opened the fridge and grabbed a couple of bottles of water.

Mom scoffed.

"All I'm saying is that it's a rough age, Drea. Be kind and considerate to yourself and others. That's how you were raised." Mom walked into the dining room with the platter. I hung back.

If I was being honest, everything *was* weird, but it wasn't something I could talk about with anyone. There was too much at risk, and I already knew what the consequences of change could be—look at what had happened between me and Olivia. I took a deep breath and walked in to join everyone. The rest of the night was easy; we ate and laughed, and I got out of my own head. We took pictures for our socials and some with my parents.

After our FaceTime with Vanessa and Faye, Olivia was indeed the first to leave. She somehow said goodbye to everyone but me, but I didn't care. Some truce. She could do whatever she wanted. She even hugged my mom, and I saw her wipe away a few tears. Later, Mom wouldn't tell me what they had talked about.

"Some things just aren't your business," she said after everyone was gone and we were cleaning up. I sighed, letting it go. Mom kissed the top of my forehead before she walked away to finish packing. I packed too, enough for four days, because I knew my mother—three days was going to turn into four. As I finished, Hailee texted.

> Hails: Tonight was fun, A! I'm picking you up tomorrow at 12. Don't get in the car if you don't have the face masks with you.
> Andrea: I should take them out on principle.
> Hails: You're so cute when you pretend I won't get my way.
> Andrea: You're the worst.
> Hails: I love you. Goodnight, see you tomorrow.
> Andrea: Dream of me lol.
> Hails: I always do.

I slammed my phone down on the bed and blew out a breath. I really shouldn't be saying things like that anymore;

I was just asking for heartbreak and disappointment. What I should have been doing was trying to prepare myself for a long weekend at Hailee's house, now that I couldn't look at her without wanting to run my hands through her hair, or hold her hand, or kiss her lips. I opened up my social media.

> @DreaWArt: I'm staying at @HaileeTxo's for a few days this week. We're going to do a Q&A on Instagram for my mom's website at 8PM EST. Send in your questions!

I woke up to the doorbell ringing. I picked up my phone to look at the time. 8:30 a.m. My parents were probably already gone. The doorbell kept ringing. I figured it was a solicitor and was absolutely going to go back to sleep when Hailee texted me that she was outside. I slunk down the stairs and opened the door.

"Hey Drea," she said easily. Her hair was curled and pinned back in the middle; she wore jean shorts and a crisp white shirt, and was looking at me expectantly. I stepped aside to let her in.

"Why are you here so early, Hails?" I asked. I was too tired to be self-conscious about the sleep in my voice. Seconds ticked by on the clock in the foyer hallway. I was slightly comforted by it.

"I was hoping we could talk," Hailee said. I started toward the living room but she called my name to stop me, motioning toward the steps. My parents were definitely gone by now, so we didn't have to, but I went with it. Once we got to my room, I sat down on my unmade bed while Hailee sat in my chair. I looked out of the window to the left of me, the sky looking a little dark even though it was morning. It was going to rain.

"What's up?" I asked. Hailee's mouth opened and closed a few times at first without her saying anything. She was clearly struggling to find the words. I'd been there, especially around her these past few weeks. I adjusted the way I sat and waited until she was ready

"I'm sorry Drea. I . . . I don't want to be your friend anymore," Hailee said.

"What?" I asked, though I'd heard her clearly. The room felt like it was starting to spin.

"I don't want to be your friend anymore. It's all too much," Hailee continued, Her mouth was set in that firm line, her feet shoulder-length apart, ready for a fight. She seemed as though she were looking past me, and I reached out for her heart, her hand, something to keep her. She moved just out of my grasp. I watched as she unclasped her hands and put them neatly at her sides. I began to cry, pulling my bottom lip inside to avoid making noise. I realized it was the same way I had cried when Olivia ended our friendship years ago.

"What's too much?" I asked, going through our last nine years of friendship in my mind, playing a slideshow of moments where I could've been too much. I was coming up empty. I wasn't perfect, sure, but this was the first time she'd ever complained to me about anything.

"All of it. The constant need to take breaks; the stares we get when we're together because people want to stop and ask you questions. It's all embarrassing. Don't you get that?" Hailee asked. Her hands at her hips, her mouth in a scowl. She scoffed at me, but as she pointed her finger in my face, she became Olivia—her hair back in its high ponytail, her face flushed with anger as she closed the rest of the space between us, a sinister smile on her lips.

"Well, if you feel that way, we don't have to be friends!" I shouted back. I was twelve again, and Olivia and I were in the hallway of our middle school, paint splattered all over our clothes, trying to hurt each other.

"I don't want to be friends with a person who can't keep secrets anyway," Olivia spat.

"What is happening? Why are you doing this? Because I told the truth?" I yelled. "Your parents *did* leave you alone for two weeks. We were trying to help you—me, my mom, and my dad." A crowd was forming around us now. To the right of me, Charlie, Fiona, and Hailee were watching us. Horrified.

"Oh, you just act like your life is perfect. Perfect Andrea and her perfect family, with a mom and dad who love her. It doesn't make you better than me," Olivia snarled.

"Yes, it does. I hate you and I always will," I shot back, tears streaming faster down my face. The kids in the hall began to laugh, so loudly I covered my ears. I was seventeen once more as I looked around me, but the laughter grew louder and louder. I closed my eyes to try and block out the sound. When I opened them again, I was back in my room with Hailee.

"I'm sorry, Drea, I love you, but I'll never be *in* love with you." she said. Her hair was drawn back into a single braid, her eyes looking sad but clearly full of pity. She reached forward and patted my shoulder like a parent trying to console a child. As she pulled her hand back, I grasped for it, and we both looked down. Then she yanked hers out of mine and bit her lip.

"Okay, okay, that's fine. We can be friends then," I pleaded. "Just don't leave." Tears began streaming down my face and I ignored the stinging in my legs, begging me to sit down. I was afraid to move.

"Well, now it's too awkward to stay," Hailee said with one final, curt nod, then walked out of my room. She didn't look back.

I woke up in a cold sweat in the middle of summer. My heart raced as I checked my phone and saw that it was only 4:00 a.m. I took a few deep breaths and gave myself permission to go back to sleep.

~~~

I woke up again early enough to say goodbye to my parents and remind them about their promise. I locked the door behind them and got dressed in my painting overalls before making breakfast. Then, I connected my phone to the house speakers and started blasting music. I walked out to the patio and situated myself in front of my portrait. For the third year, I was entering the art showcase held at Steamworks—this huge industrial creative space—toward the end of the summer. I had lost the previous two, and each loss gutted me, but this year I had something to prove: I was going to win. Something was off, though, about the self-portrait I was planning to submit—and I couldn't figure out what. The sun slid in to cradle the right side of my face, so I stopped painting to ask it a question.

"Why is this not working?"

When the sun had no answer for me, I sighed and sat down on one of the patio chairs. Maybe I didn't know myself well enough to do this self-portrait. What I did know for sure was that I needed to figure it out before the showcase. After a few more paint strokes, I packed up my supplies and brought the easel and work back inside. When I came down to lock the back-patio doors, the front doorbell actually rang. I opened the door to find Hailee in a flowy, white maxi skirt and a jean crop top.

"I could not do jeans today," Hailee said, bursting inside. We walked together to lock the patio doors and back into the living room.

"I'm already packed—let me just change really quick," I said, heading toward the stairs.

"Okay, I'll come with you," Hailee called. She started to follow me out of the living room and I panicked. The last thing either of us needed was to make my earlier dream a reality.

"No!" I said, a little louder than I needed to. Hailee took a step back. I smiled as fast as I could and clarified, "No, there's no need. Stay here . . . I'll be down in a flash." I took off toward the steps and didn't groan in embarrassment until I was upstairs with the door closed behind me. I changed as quickly as I was able, berating myself the entire time.

I pulled my suitcase down the steps, holding the railing in order to keep my balance. This took me longer than it would have if I'd asked Hailee for help, but I didn't want help. Sometimes, things take longer when I do them, but I just want to do them on my own. Hailee met me at the bottom of the stairs and I let her take the suitcase then. I set the house alarm, pressed a button on my phone to turn off every light, and we left.

When we reached the street that Hailee lived on, I watched her as she turned down the music, pulled into the driveway, and took the keys out of the ignition without looking at me. I watched the street for a few moments—cars drove leisurely past us, their windows down playing a variety of music we could only catch snippets of. Hailee didn't even acknowledge it. A conversation was brewing.

"Are we okay, Andrea?" Hailee asked, finally turning to me. She set the keys down on the center console. For the first time in a long time, if I was being honest with myself, I wasn't sure. Here we sat, this big secret between us, but one I was intent on keeping. I remained silent as Hailee tucked a piece of hair behind her ear and blew out a breath. The sun tucked itself behind a cloud, maybe unsure where this was going either. "Because we don't feel okay. If I did something wrong, please let me know so I can fix it."

Oh no. She thought she had done something wrong, when I was the one who wasn't being honest. After her face fell, I decided I couldn't take it. I reached for Hailee's hand and squeezed it.

"We're great, Hails. I'm spending the weekend with my best friend, and later we're heading to the thrift shop pop-up. The first BSE activity!" I cheered. We locked eyes and grinned at each other before I got out of the car and she followed suit. I opened the back-seat door and took my suitcase out. Leaving it standing, I ran around the car to hug Hailee. We stayed like that for a long moment before I spoke again. "I am sorry I made you question us. What did we say when we were twelve? You and me, we're good like—"

"Cheese and pep. Pep and cheese," Hailee finished, smiling wide and pulling me close again, her laughter at the edge of my ear. I joined her in it. Hailee grabbed my face with her hands as she pulled back, winking before letting me go.

She walked around the car and grabbed my suitcase. After I got the keys and locked the door, I watched as the sun peeked back out from behind the clouds. I shook my head fondly. The sun, not a fan of possible confrontation—noted.

Once inside, I sat on the bench by the door and removed my sneakers. Hailee stood beside me and tossed off her flip-flops with ease. We walked in step as she wheeled my suitcase into her room. I could hear her mom come out into the living room.

"Hey Mama Janice," I called as I walked over to hug her, once we were back. I let Janice hug me like we hadn't just seen each other days ago. When we were at arm's length, she bopped my nose. Janice really was the best "second mom" ever. She was always making me laugh (that's where Hailee got it from). Sure, she was a terrible cook, but sleepovers at Hailee's always meant we got to have whatever takeout food my parents thought could be done better at home. Mama J is an artist too, so we always talked about art at our biweekly Saturday dinner, and in the mornings after sleepovers while Hailee slept in.

"Sweet rings, Mama J," I complimented, letting her squeeze me one more time before letting go.

"Thank you, sweet pea. They didn't turn out how I wanted, but I love them." The rings were all silver save for a different-colored jewel at the center of each. Beside them gleamed her wedding band, the one she still wore to keep her husband close to her heart. Hailee's dad had died a year before our families met. "You like? We can make some on Tuesday if you want?"

"I would! Very much," I exclaimed. Hailee and I had been trying to get her to start selling her jewelry for years. Janice laughed.

"Can I have my best friend back?" Hailee asked. She pouted playfully and grabbed my arm. "Ma, we'll be home in time for dinner. I'll send pictures." She let go of my arm and then offered hers out to me.

Janice smiled. She had pinned her hair back today, probably to keep it out of her face while she worked. She cupped Hailee's face gently, and I watched as Hailee rolled her eyes but then leaned into her mother's hand, smiling as Janice kissed her cheek.

"Drive safe, have fun. Say hi to the girls for me!" Mama J said as she ushered us out the door.

We were one street over and at a red light when Hailee looked at me like she had a big idea. I turned down the radio and gave her my full attention.

"I think I want a back tattoo. Like a bird or something," Hailee theorized, tapping her fingers on the steering wheel to the beat and ignoring my shocked expression. She looked over at me once more before the light turned green, then huffed, "Oh, cut the dramatics. I could if I wanted to."

"What would you even get? A bald eagle?" I asked, laughing as we pulled up in front of the shop and spotted Fiona, Olivia, and Charlie waiting for us.

"You are the worst. You know bloody well that I could pull it off, don't you?" Hailee protested, undoing her seat belt and getting out of the car.

"Bloody well!" I mimicked, joining her. We walked over to the girls before she spoke again.

"Shut up! Charlie got me hooked on a new British show!" Hailee swatted at me playfully as Charlie shrugged triumphantly. I hugged everyone one by one, but as I reached my arms out to Olivia, I hesitated after our confrontation last night—though not before noticing the look of horror on her face, and, if I wasn't seeing things, disappointment when I pulled away. Weird. Hailee had asked me to keep trying with her, though, so I would. With a small smile Olivia's way, I stepped to the side and let her pass into the store.

Once we got inside, a very pretty Black woman greeted us, literally bouncing with excitement. Her braids were past her butt and she was wearing a black-and-white rocker tee of a band I didn't know, with dark-blue jeans and Doc Martens. A tall Asian woman who stood beside her smiled too, but she was more reserved.

"Welcome to As You Are, where you can dress your best for less!" the Black woman said with full excitement. I looked around and saw rows and rows of clothes categorized by style and mood. My mom would love it here. I looked to the right of me and saw rows and rows of shoes too, and, to my delight, a place to sit to try them on.

"Don't mind her excitement, I'm Sarah, and this is Hillary. You're our first customers and we just hope you like the place," Sarah said. She was wearing a floral dress, a pleather jacket, and the same pair of Docs as the woman beside her. They both looked young; I was terrible at guessing ages, but they both seemed like they were in their mid-to-late twenties.

"It's nice to meet you. I'm Olivia; to the right of me is Fiona; next to her is Charlie. The two people to the left of me are Hailee and Andrea. We like what we see from here. We're going to have a look around!" Olivia said with a bright smile of her own. When the two women were out of earshot, she leaned into us and spoke.

"It's like looking at Drea and Hails in a few years." I glanced over at the two women from where we stood by the jeans. Olivia wasn't wrong—a swap in styles, sure—but I could see it. I turned back to find Hailee smiling at me.

"I had to do a double take myself," Fiona added, picking up a pair of distressed jeans and holding them to her waist. She tossed them to the left of her without looking, straight into a cart that Charlie had appeared with.

"Thanks Fi, I found this dress for you," Charlie said, handing Fiona an A-line black-and-white shift dress. Fiona smiled appreciatively. Jeans were not really her thing—we had that in common—so when I'd seen her pick them up, I'd figured. But Hailee was still surprised.

"It is so wild to me when you two do that," Hailee said, looking at me to agree. I just shrugged and picked up a jean jacket with a lion on the back that was just my size. While I didn't wear them often, I could pair it with my black jeans, white Chucks, and the little gold heart necklace my mom bought for me when she was in Spain this past Easter. Olivia and Fiona added a few more shirts and dresses to the cart before I gingerly placed my jacket inside.

"Oh, Andrea and Hailee just kissed!" Charlie announced as I looked up from the clothing rack with like eight T-shirts on my arm. If I'd had water, I would've done a spit take. Charlie chuckled at my expression.

"I mean future you, over there." Charlie nodded her head toward the store owner. We all followed her line of vision and saw them canoodling with each other like there was no one else in the store. It was sweet. I ignored the pang in my chest and worked to look busy.

"Let's go look at shoes! I think I saw some cute boots for fall," Hailee said, her voice cracking on the last word.

"Smooth Hails," Olivia chuckled, pulling all of her perfectly straightened blond hair over her left shoulder. "You sound like Andrea when she's well . . . saying or doing anything." She straightened her back before she began walking toward the shoes. She smirked at me as she passed, and I fought and failed not to roll my eyes.

The next day we spent lounging around the house. The afternoon came and went while Hailee, Janice, and I watched a few episodes of *Law & Order: SVU* and some lesser procedural drama before Janice decided it was time for dinner. I really loved being in their home, watching them banter. You could hear the love in their back-and-forth: the trust, the care.

"Girls, dinner is ready!" Janice called out. While we ate, conversation was easy. We spent the meal talking about how excited we were for the art show in ShoeHorn the next morning. Our second item to complete on the list. We even planned to make rings with Janice when we got back.

"Hey Mom, we have to start the Live for Mama Ev's Instagram," Hailee said a little later, from where we all sat on the couch. My back was propped up by pillows that were against the armrest. Hailee sat on the opposite end, her back against the other armrest. Janice sat in the middle with her feet firmly planted on the carpet. Hailee and I watched for a few more moments, then we stood to leave.

"Okay, have fun. I'll be watching," Janice said. She looked at us for a moment and smiled. "You know, I am hip."

"If you were as hip as you thought, you wouldn't be saying the word *hip*," Hailee reminded, and Janice pouted. "Love you too."

I reapplied my red lipstick and Hailee fixed her hair when we got back into her room. Hailee set up her laptop on the far end of her bed, so we'd be in frame. I walked around to sit to the left of Hailee since my left side was my strongest. Once I was situated, I pulled out my phone and opened the Notes app, where I had put the questions I wanted to answer.

"Ready?" Hailee asked. I nodded and Hailee started the video. "Hey you lovely people! Thanks for joining our Insta Live and asking us questions." We smiled at the camera. The rush of excitement that came with being in front of the camera hit, and I smiled wider.

When my mom asked us if we'd do a Live for Evelyn Williams Designs, to reach younger customers, we said yes immediately. I loved being in front of a camera, and Hailee negotiated a few extra cookies and a free outfit before she said yes. The initial plan was to do the Live with my mom, but when she and Dad had to rush to NYC, she gave us permission to do it ourselves as long as Mama Janice watched on her own phone.

"We're going to go back and forth answering different questions you asked us on our Instagram Stories earlier. I hope no one made it too weird," I laughed.

"Let's get started," Hailee said, looking at me and winking. A nice reminder that Hailee and I were fine. I scrunched my nose at her and looked back at the computer.

"Okay, the first question I get a lot. The question is, *What's it like being the daughter of a famous fashion icon?*

"I mean it's pretty great. She is funny, smart, talented, cool, and all the things you think she would be but . . . she is still very much my mom first. She embarasses me at school drop offs, tells corny mom jokes and then laughs at them, is terrible at using emojis, and uses the word 'Sup' unironically, but . . ."

"But we love her very much," Hailee jumped in. "Next question?"

*"What's your favorite design of your mom's?*

"I like her dresses, they always have pockets! What about you, Hails?"

"I like the Andrea jumpsuit," Hailee shrugged. "It also has pockets, you can dress it up or down, and it's named after my favorite person. It's a win, win!" she finished, her eyes on me momentarily as she bumped my shoulder.

"Flattery will get you everywhere. Okay, this next question asks: *Will your mom ever design menswear or formalwear at all? I think she would be so good at it.*

"Honestly, me too. I don't know if she has any plans to, but that would be fun! Prom for us will be here someday and I'd love to wear one of my mom's designs," I said. "And between you and me? I hope she's watching because I've got ideas."

"Getting in there early, Drea? I respect it. You'd look great in a midnight blue dress with sparkles," Hailee added, her smile genuine. We watched each other for a few moments, and it felt like the world had stopped. Hailee bit her lip and pressed her hand onto the bed. "You're going to look so pretty no matter what, I know it." I squealed internally, then cleared my throat and turned back to the camera.

"This next question is very sweet. Someone wants to know when did we meet?" I looked back to Hailee, knowing how much she loved to tell this story. Hailee leaned into the camera like she was getting ready to spill a secret. I couldn't take my eyes off of her. I loved the way she could be both charming and personable; how everyone who knew her, loved her.

"We met at a neighborhood potluck when we were nine. Mama J and I had just moved to the neighborhood, and when we got there, Andrea came bouncing over to introduce herself. She had the cutest white bows in her hair—"

"It was a whole thing. I went through a phase," I interjected, leaning forward.

"It was the cutest and she was so friendly. We hit it off immediately and have been best friends ever since." Hailee looked back at me with a smile. "Okay folks, the last question is: *Are your parents as close as you two are?*"

"Yes, Mama and Daddy Williams love Mama J," I reassured. "Not as much as I do of course. Shout out to Mama J who is watching." I smiled and waved at the camera.

"She's such a suck-up, you guys," Hailee teased, waving at the camera anyway. "Hi Mom!"

Hailee threw an arm over my shoulder and pulled me in. I smiled into the embrace and wrapped my arm around her waist.

"Bye everyone! Thanks for hanging out with us," I said.

"Later!" Hailee followed, ending the livestream with a click.

Hailee got up from the bed and put her laptop back on her desk. I tried not to miss the contact. I stood up too and paced around the room to stretch my legs. There were pictures everywhere. One of the other things I loved most about Hailee was her obsession with capturing moments. There were so many moments in her room.

On the dresser sat the lucky cat her dad had bought her, when they'd gone back to China to visit family, two years before he died. Next to the lucky cat, a picture of her mother, pregnant with her, alongside her father. A picture of her grandma (her dad's mother) and the best-friend bracelets Charlie made last summer on her dresser. On the wall to the right, pictures of Hailee and me next to a set of Hailee with each of the girls: Fiona, Charlie, and Olivia. In the far-left corner was a bookshelf with spines coordinated by color; I spotted her volume of Chinese poetry, the one I knew was dogeared the most. Her grandmother (her mom's mother) had given it to her. Now, when they talked on the phone, they only spoke Chinese, and Hailee said it made her feel closer to her. Against the far wall was a shelf filled with the gifts my family had given her over the years: knickknacks from my mom's travels, "I saw this and thought of you" gifts from me, and ceramic cookies for her birthday last year from Dad. On the far wall next to the shelf was the portrait of Hailee that I'd painted. I stopped pacing to look at it.

"I still can't believe you took the time to do that," Hailee said, coming to stand beside me.

"It was nothing," I brushed off. I'm not great at taking compliments about my art. Maybe because it meant so much to me, but I worried that some people (not the girls of course) were only saying they liked it because of my mom. No one ever said as much to me directly, but, I worried still. Maybe this summer—aside from being the best one ever—would also help me accept the praise I was given.

"Except, I know that it was something. I know how much work they took. You did one for all of us. And they're beautiful."

"Thank you, Hail."

"You still haven't given Olivia hers yet, have you?" she asked.

"No," I replied. "And I don't know what I'm so scared of." Oh, you know, a bear attack, showing up to school completely naked, rejection . . . the usual. The truth was, I didn't know *how* to give Olivia hers. It was nothing like the others.

"You will. I know it's complicated, but I bet she'd love it. Instead of just letting her think that she doesn't have one," Hailee finished, still not taking her eyes off the picture.

"You want to know something else?" I asked. My heart was beating fast inside my chest. The streetlights danced outside of her window, and a horn honked incessantly.

"Sure."

"Yours is my favorite," I said. Hailee smiled with pride. She grabbed my hand and squeezed it again.

"You're trying to make me cry," Hailee said plainly. "And if I cry, my makeup will be ruined, and I won't be able to capture this moment. Would you really sabotage greatness?"

"You are so dramatic. I'm going to go shower," I said. I needed to breathe. I grabbed my shower caddy, towel, and pajamas and left the room. But I waited behind the door. I don't know what I was waiting for, but when I thought I heard a little groan from her, I couldn't hide my disappointment. Was being with me that frustrating? My mere company enough to make her groan in annoyance?

By the time I was out of the shower, though, I was ready to let go of whatever the groan meant. Who was I to harp when I was the one saying the wrong things all day, because I couldn't say the one thing I was desperate to say? The walk back to Hailee's room was easy. I said goodnight to Mama J, and texted my parents goodnight too.

"Water was hot?" Hailee asked, pulling her hair into a loose ponytail and drawing back her side of the covers to climb in.

"Deliciously so," I said, pulling on my satin sleep cap and climbing under my side of the covers. When we were both in bed, we moved to face each other. "Worst part of today?"

"Your singing on the way here," Hailee teased.

"Hey! I am under the weather . . . that's why I wasn't on my A game today," I offered. After an unconvincing cough, Hailee nodded as if it were true, and I laughed again.

"Favorite part of today?" Hailee asked. She scooted closer to me and for the first time in a long time, I thought nothing of it.

"The food was great, and the livestream too. What about you?" I asked, whispering the last part as Hailee reached up to shut off the light.

"This. This is my favorite part of today," she answered. She moved to lie on her back so she could stare at the ceiling. When we were kids, I'd helped Hailee beg Mama J to put the glow-in-the-dark stars on the ceiling. They'd stayed there until Hailee turned twelve and decided they were too childish. She kept five of the tiniest ones up on the ceiling, though, to represent our friend group. But something looked different from the last time I was here. Were two of the stars closer to each other than the others?

I remained on my side, turning my head away from the ceiling to watch the streetlights dance across Hailee's face through the gaps of the curtain on the window. I closed my eyes and opened them again. This was my favorite part of the day too. I couldn't say it out loud, but I could think it, and that had to be enough. I was going to make it enough. While Hailee launched into the story of the most recent conversation she'd had with her grandmother, I counted her freckles. I got to thirty-two before Hailee turned to face me again.

"This is our first big summer adventure. Are you nervous at all to keep doing the list?" she asked, chewing on her lip. I nodded, moving my left arm to sit atop the covers.

"Definitely, but I think the nerves are half the fun. And we'll be doing it together. I got you," I promised. I really was determined to make sure that this summer was the one we'd reference when we were old and gray, when our grandkids would ask us what we were like when we were their age. Was I nervous? Sure, but more excited than anything. Completing this list with Hailee by my side was going to be a breeze, and we were going to have memories that lasted a lifetime, and moments worthy of the gallery that was Hailee's room.

"Love you, A," Hailee said, before turning away from me.

"You too," I replied. I turned so that my back was to Hailee's, and fell asleep to the sounds of her even breathing.

Someone knocked three times before entering. I opened one eye and then the other. I felt Hailee groan against my neck. I looked down and saw that her arm was around my waist. Had we fallen asleep like that? No. I was pretty sure that it happened in the middle of the night. Did I reach for Hailee first? Or was it the other way around? Regardless, I really needed to pee. When I looked out of the corner of my eye, I saw Janice and screamed. I scrambled to get out of the bed. Hailee groaned.

"Andrea!"

"Sorry."

"Good morning, sweetie," Janice said to me, but I kept looking over at the spot I had just occupied. Hailee sat up, her ponytail skewed to the right and drool on the sides of her mouth.

"Mom, you gotta knock," Hailee drowsed, her eyes still closed as though she were trying to hold on to sleep. I stood still, afraid to make a sound. Truthfully, I was mortified—had Mama J witnessed our cuddling? We were just sleeping, and Hailee's aunt Wendy is gay, but . . . you never know.

"I did, three times. We're going to have to grab breakfast on the road since we're running late," Janice said. In my peripheral I could tell that her eyes were on me, but they were gentle. Her hands were clasped neatly in front of her. Her eyebrow raised—my mom must've taught her about the eyebrow raise. I still didn't know where to look. Hailee huffed once more and got up.

"Fine, but I have to go shower," Hailee grumbled and left the room. I finally looked at Janice, who smiled sweetly. Something was coming.

"You know you're my second daughter, right, sweetie?" Janice said. She motioned for me to sit, and I obliged; it was best to rest when we'd end up doing a lot of walking today, anyway.

"Yes, I know. You're my bonus mom," I replied.

Janice nodded her head in agreement and pounced.

"Now that we have established that, I want you to know that I love you both so much, and if you two were . . . of course, there would be new rules about closed doors, but—"

"Uh. It wasn't what it looked like. We're not anything. I promise!" I spoke up. I looked down at my pizza-print-covered socks.

"But if you were, I'd be okay with it. I'd be happy, even," Janice said, grabbing my hands and squeezing them. Her smile was wide and her gaze supportive. Her black hair, cut in a bob, moved quickly as she nodded her head yes again. I leaned in and let her kiss my cheek.

"Happy about what?" Hailee asked, walking back into the room with a towel wrapped around her. I looked up at Janice with a watery smile. Janice looked back at me with a question in her eyes. *Have you told her how you feel?* I shook my head silently, but Janice hugged me anyway.

"Nothing," we said quickly. I stood up and grabbed my clothes.

"I'll change in the bathroom," I said. I didn't wipe my tears until I was in there with the door closed. I had vowed not to spend the summer pining over my best friend, and now here I was still doing it and crying silently to her mother.

~~~

Thirty minutes later, that mother was now stealing glances at me as we drove in the car. Hailee, none the wiser, sang along to the songs coming from my aux cord, in between our selfies that I leaned forward for, grazing Hailee's arm and shoulder as she made sure that I was in the frame. As we decided which ones to post, Janice pulled into the breakfast drive-thru.

"I want—" Hailee started, but Janice cut her off. She smiled over at her daughter.

"This is not my first time at the rodeo." Janice turned back to the speaker. "Hello, I'll have four breakfast burritos; a ham, egg, and cheese sandwich; three hash browns; two waters; and an orange juice." Hailee applauded and I laughed in the back seat. We got our food and drove for twenty more minutes before we reached the outdoor art show. Janice parked and we made our way to the start. White tents lined the streets, which had been blocked off for the next two hours. I couldn't stop the smile spreading across my face. I wasn't sure where we would begin, but I was truly in my element. The three of us walked by a few tents, talking to each vendor, and I promised to circle back to a couple later to talk about technique. When we reached the end of the first row, Janice stopped.

"What if we split up?" she asked. She smiled at me as I nodded. Hailee watched us for a moment.

"Okay, cool. Mom, we have our phones. We'll meet back here in an hour?" she asked.

"I was thinking we could hang for a bit and Andrea could explore on her own," Janice clarified. Hailee looked at her quizzically, adjusting the small backpack straps on her shoulder.

"I'd like that," I said. Leaving them would allow me to clear my head and get lost in art for a while, instead of spending so much time thinking about Hailee. Space would do us both some good. I was completely grateful for Mama J's understanding.

"Why? That's silly," Hailee answered. She looked over at me, silently asking if I was upset. I shook my head no. I smiled in an effort to reassure her. Hailee didn't look convinced, but she conceded. "Okay, I guess we'll see you in an hour."

Hailee hesitated after she spoke. She smiled, but I knew it wasn't genuine. Her issue had to do with the abruptness of the decision. I was assuming that, anyway, because it was the only thing that made sense. We set our alarms to an hour from that moment, then I switched my phone to the front pocket of my jeans. I waved goodbye and started down the next street.

I bought a few things small enough to carry in the tote that I'd brought with me. I avoided the paints, because they would be my "sorry to break tradition" gift in a few days. I stood in line to buy a sandwich I could eat while walking. The person in front of me was taking forever to decide what they wanted. It was hard to tell from behind, but as I waited, I realized this person looked a lot like George Fallon. The unusually tiny ears were my biggest clue.

"I'll have the meatball sub," George decided, finally. I snickered as the workers sighed in relief. He turned around and looked at me quizzically, before sliding into his signature smirk that half the girls in school went lovesick over.

"Next," the worker called. George stepped aside, but didn't leave. I ignored the way he kept smiling as I ordered. I was not going to be one of the girls who swooned just because he showed them attention. I was so determined not to give him a reaction that I lost my footing when I was done and stumbled into George instead.

"First she makes fun of me, then she can't get enough of me," George teased, placing his hands on either side of my arms to steady me. Mortified wasn't a sufficient enough word. I didn't care what he thought of me, but it was still embarrassing that my cerebral palsy meant my balance was trash.

"Sorry," I said sincerely, stepping out of his arms. I watched him turn to grab his order. I assumed the conversation would end here, and he would leave, but instead he kept standing there looking down like I was a puzzle to figure out.

"Don't worry about it," George said easily. He grabbed my sandwich before I could move and handed it to me. I smiled to signal that I was done with the conversation, and began to walk away, intent on not missing out on any good deals, but he fell in step beside me. "I know what you can do to make it up to me."

"I fell into you; I didn't stain your T-shirt or anything," I said, taking a bite of my sandwich as we walked. I could still feel his eyes on me, and I wasn't sure what his endgame was, but I didn't know if I could trust him.

"Same thing," George replied, lengthening his stride to keep up. "You walk faster than I thought. Slow down."

"What is that supposed to mean? So you think that because I'm disabled, I can't walk fast?" I stopped in front of a table to get a better look.

"I-I didn't mean to imply that, at all. You just walk faster than I was expecting, " George said. He took a bite of his sub and I watched as he began talking to the vendor in front of us. He bought a couple figurines, and the vendor wrapped them carefully and placed them in a bag, clearly smitten. "Anything for your girlfriend?' she asked.

"We're not—" I started.

"Anything you'd like, babe." George winked, like we were playing some game. I rolled my eyes and looked at the woman, ready to tell her, "No, thank you." And that's when I saw it. A tiny, cerulean music box in the back corner of her booth. Hailee would love it.

"Is that for sale?" I asked, pointing. The way the sun shone on the box only made me long for it more. I bit the inside of my cheek as I waited. I could already see the joy on Hailee's face when I gave it to her later. She'd cry a little, we'd hug, and I would be forgiven for needing to take some space from her today. Space wasn't a thing that we did normally. We could if we wanted to, but . . . we never wanted to. At least, until I realized that I wanted more with Hailee than I was ever going to get.

Now, here I was with George of all people, who I still didn't trust completely but who was turning out to be not the worst company.

"Yes, and the music still plays. Fifteen dollars," the vendor said. I moved to pull the money out of my purse, but George spoke first.

"Babe, I said I got it. Thank you, Penny," he said, and handed her the money. Penny wrapped the music box with the same care. Then she placed it into a small bag and handed it to me. I placed it carefully in my tote and thanked her.

"Bye, Penny. I'll swing back by later." George waved and we moved on. We passed three more tables in a strangely comfortable silence, before my curiosity broke it.

"What is your endgame exactly, walking around with me and letting these people think we are a couple?" I asked. George ignored the question at first, but then pointed out a bench.

"Let's sit over there for a sec. I am tired of walking and eating," he answered, already heading toward the bench. I followed him reluctantly, but I knew the break would be nice on my legs. We sat and finished the rest of our sandwiches.

After he swallowed his last bite, George offered: "I have no endgame. I am just curious about you, Andrea."

"Why now?" I asked. Guys like George didn't just wake up one day and decide to be curious about girls like me. The sudden change made me skeptical. This was not about to be some *She's All That* sequence of events, not on my watch. George had to want something from me, and I was determined to figure out what it was before I said no and sent him on his way. I knew being nosy was going to come back to bite me someday—just not today.

"Because you were alone finally. Every time I see you, you're with Hailee or one of the others. You and Hailee are practically joined at the hip. I can't really talk to you in the way

I want to like that. They say three is a crowd . . ." George trailed off, decidedly making direct eye contact with me as he spoke. His eyes really were the perfect shade of green. I was beginning to understand the appeal. Ugh. He smirked again.

"Do I have something on my face?" he asked with a wide smile. I shook my head no. "I'm not complaining, but you were staring pretty hard."

"Shut up," I groaned, though I knew I didn't have a leg to stand on with this one. He really was cute; it was unnerving. Still: "I'm sorry but I don't buy that."

"Buy what?" George asked. He ran a hand through his hair and it flopped to the other side adorably. I shouldn't be finding anything he did adorable, but the longer he looked at me like I was something to behold, the harder I found it to resist his charms.

"That you always wanted to talk to me, but couldn't because I was with Hailee."

"I don't know what the deal is between you and Olivia, but ask her. She'll tell you," George replied simply. He shrugged his shoulders and looked away. I chewed on that information and watched other people pass us by.

"Well, I'm here now. What do you want to know?" I watched his face light up as he turned back to me. And I realized at that moment—with the noise of art vendors and patrons swelling around us, the perfect gifts in my tote bag, the pull of summer sun, and the hum of curiosity between us— that he was the perfect candidate to fulfill the secret item on my list. He could help me fall out of love with Hailee—and *into* it with him. I could still keep my best friend.

"You are, and I'm glad," George winked again. The intensity behind his stare was surprising, so I looked past him for a moment. I watched a man haggle with a woman for her art. This wasn't a flea market for crying out loud. The man walked away in a huff before I trained my eyes back on George. "How did you get into art? You're the best artist in the class."

"Thank you, that's very sweet. I got into it when we were kids. My mom took Hailee and me to New York and I loved the clothes, of course, but I was fascinated by the graffiti on the streets and the art at the museums we visited. I've been painting ever since." I smiled fondly at the memory.

"I don't have a creative bone in my body," George joked, but I could maybe see some real insecurity behind it. I felt an intense urge to correct him. During the school year, I'd seen him play soccer when Olivia dragged us to the boy's games, so she could secretly keep her eye on the coach's son—Jamie Gold—who was the equipment manager. After the third game, I'd realized Olivia had only looked at the field once. When I pulled her aside to ask about it, she clammed up but recovered quickly, insisting she had no idea what I was talking about since he was just her history tutor.

"Soccer takes a lot of creativity actually. The girls and I have seen you play. I know it's not easy being the star player," I said. George shrugged and cast his eyes down. I was tempted to place a reassuring hand on his shoulder. I stopped myself at the last second.

"You have? Actually . . . I saw you a few times with Olivia and the others. She stopped coming to the games for a while, and she thought none of us noticed how she watched Jamie on the sidelines more than the game itself," George chuckled. It made me a little dizzy as he smiled over at me. He leaned toward me conspiratorially. "Who were you there to see?"

"I was there for Jamie too," I smiled. I laughed behind my hand as he pouted. "I'm kidding. We went for Olivia."

"You're lucky that you're so cute," George said. He bit his lip and left me to flounder for a second.

"I am?" I asked, mostly myself, but George heard me.

"Cuter and cuter by the second." The wind picked up and I tried to smooth my hair back down. He reached up to do it for me, then paused when he realized what he was doing. "Sorry."

"It's okay, I've got it," I said, my phone alarm going off suddenly. I pulled it out and shut it off. "And I have to go. I'm meeting back up with Hailee."

I stood up, wiping my hands on my jeans. George stood too, his face falling.

"Ah. Well . . . this was really fun," he said, stuffing his hands in his pockets. We stood there staring at each other. I was sadder to go than I'd expected.

"It was. See you around, George." I turned to leave.

"Wait," he called out, grabbing my hand. I turned around, surprised. "Let's do this again. Give me your phone?" He smiled and it eased my immediate reluctance. I contemplated for a moment, then shrugged, handing my phone over. He gave me his and I put my number and name in. We returned our phones to their respective owners and George took my hand again.

"I really should go," I said. George pouted and we laughed. I promised to answer when he texted, and he smiled again. It really was a nice smile. He stepped toward me and now we were inches apart; my head was spinning.

"Don't friends hug goodbye?" he asked, grabbing my right hand. He didn't grab it like it was glass. He grabbed it just like he had my left. I liked that.

"Are we friends?" I whispered, looking up into his eyes.

"I'd like to be," George replied easily, closing the distance even more. I was momentarily panicked that he'd kiss me. I wasn't ready for that. Instead, we hugged for a moment longer than most friends. Once we parted, I smiled again. He waved goodbye, but didn't move, and as I walked away—for real this time—I knew he was watching and I wasn't self-conscious about it.

When I got back to the meeting spot, Hailee was standing there with her hand on her hip and Mama J was trying her best to warn me, but the daze I was in from my past hour had other plans. I came to as Hailee and her mother exchanged looks, the scowl on Hailee's face deepening. I looked at Mama J and raised an eyebrow. She mouthed, *Late*, and I nodded my head in understanding. Hailee hated being late—it was her thing. Sure, she might be a little huffy for a while, but she'd be over it by the time we got to the car. I smiled at Hailee, who was still mid-huff. She was so cute. Janice spoke first.

"You two ready to head out?" she asked. We nodded and began walking toward the exit. Hailee remained quiet as we reached the car. She climbed into the back next to me and put on her seat belt. Maybe we were making progress. Janice climbed into the driver's seat, started the car, and turned the radio up immediately. I sang along to a few songs and stole glances at Hailee, who was on her phone. She might need a little nudging. I pulled my phone out and texted her.

> Andrea: How long are you going to be mad at me for being late? I'm sorry ☺
> Hails: You think I'm mad because you were late?
> Andrea: Aren't you?
> Hails: You know what? I'm not even mad at all, don't worry about it.
> Andrea: Hails, seriously. I can't fix it if I don't know what I did.
> Hails: We'll talk about it later. I don't want to here.
> Andrea: Okay.

Hailee put her phone down and turned toward the window. I watched the back of her head until a text alert went off on my phone.

> G: Hey, it's Jamie. I just wanted to say I love you.

I laughed out loud. Hailee shot a look at me and then stared back out of the window.

Andrea: Jamie? It's too soon for love.

G: You're right. We should just be friends. My friend
   George, he's great.

Andrea: A little full of himself, no?

I couldn't stop the smile spreading across my face. I
turned my head toward Hailee, who I realized was watching
me again.

"Who are you talking to?" Hailee asked.

"No one," I replied. I bit my lip at the lie, but I wasn't
ready to share this yet. We were in the middle of something,
so, I would tell her after. I smiled at Hailee and waited until
she turned away before I unlocked my phone again.

G: I had a lot of fun today. Can we do it again?

Andrea: You must really like art shows.

G: I really like you.

Andrea: You're not so bad yourself.

G: I can work with that. I gotta go. But I'll text
   you later.

I put my phone down and turned toward my own window. Janice pulled into the driveway of their house, but didn't
move to undo her seat belt.

"I'm going to the grocery store. We should have home-
made subs for dinner. Be back in a bit," she announced. I
couldn't blame her for wanting to avoid whatever this was

going to be, because I wanted to myself. Hailee nodded her head and got out of the car. I sighed and followed suit. So, the silent treatment would remain. I prepared for battle, as dramatic as that sounds.

I matched Hailee's stride into their house, shutting the door behind us and sitting down, then taking my shoes off and waiting. Hailee slid hers off and stood up, looking me square in the eyes. She shook her head and placed her hands back on her hips.

"You needed space from me to hang out with *George Fallon*?" Hailee said. She walked past me, moving to the couch and turning on the TV. I sat there on the bench by the door, shocked. I opened and closed my mouth, before deciding that waiting was the best option. Hailee refused to look back at me.

"Hails—"

"Don't. When you said you wanted space, I was sad, but I understood. We don't always need to be joined at the hip. But ditching me for a guy? That's rich," Hailee shot out. She looked away from the television but still did not look at me. "I thought something was up. I saw you crying to my mom this morning; I figured you would tell me later. Is now a good time or . . . ?" Hailee turned the channel, but I could tell she was paying no attention.

"What? I wasn't crying," I chuckled awkwardly, walking to the other end of the couch. I'd been sure I'd done a better job hiding it than I apparently had.

"Another lie. Great. Look, I don't care if you want to hang out with George. I care that you lied to me, and you just keep doing it." She turned off the TV finally and stood, putting distance between the two of us. I remained on the couch, looking up at her.

"George and I ran into each other by total accident. It was nothing," I pleaded. Though I really didn't believe it myself. I'd had fun with George this afternoon. It was a really nice surprise. He was sweet, funny, and he apparently liked me. "How did you even find out?"

"Tracy told Lacey who told Fi who told me, because she assumed I already knew." Hailee pulled her phone out to show a picture of George and me hugging. "Tracy saw you two while she was working at the kid's craft table. Stop lying. We don't lie to each other, remember?"

"I did hang out with George, but I didn't plan to; it just happened," I said. In truth, I hated how it looked. I had needed space to clear my head and figure out how to fall out of love with the girl standing before me. I hadn't meant to make Hailee think anything else.

"It doesn't look like nothing. Do you like him?" Hailee asked, her voice cracking. Was she . . . jealous? I hated the way my heart fluttered at the thought.

"I don't know," I said honestly. I sighed when Hailee sat back down next to me. I began twiddling my thumbs. I couldn't tell her why I was hoping that I'd learn to like him, but I couldn't afford to keep lying to her either. This was excruciating. I ran a hand through my hair and looked down at the tote bag to the left of me. I gingerly pulled out the music box I'd bought for her, but kept it on my lap. We sat in silence next to each other, me on the verge of tears, and Hailee . . . well, I wasn't sure. For the first time in forever, I couldn't read her.

"I saw this and thought of you today," I started, finally. I handed Hailee the package and waited. She unwrapped the music box and gasped. Hailee looked at me, and I was so nervous and hopeful that maybe I had worried for nothing: she liked the gift, but maybe, more importantly, this could be the peace offering this moment desperately needed.

"It's beautiful," Hailee said. I breathed a sigh of relief and smiled at her. But she continued to look down at the music box. When she lifted her head, I realized she was crying. I moved to wipe the tears away, but Hailee stopped me.

"Please, don't touch me right now," she said. She stood, still holding the music box, and walked into the bathroom. I watched her go and then looked down at my shaking hands. I could feel tears at the edges of my eyes. I sucked my bottom lip into my mouth to muffle the sob. Hailee reappeared, walking past me and into her room, probably to set the music box down. When she came back to the living room, she sat further away from me, but close enough to hand me a little bag. I opened it and pulled out a figurine of a Black girl, painting. The girl sat on a blue chair and wore a pink overall set, a paintbrush in her right hand, and her hair pulled back into a loose bun. I held the figurine close to my chest.

"It's perfect," I whispered, closing my eyes and letting my own tears fall. When I opened them again, I carefully rewrapped the gift and placed it in my tote bag. After wiping the remaining tears from my face, I looked over at Hailee and laughed. "When was the last time we cried this much?"

"Your fourteenth birthday, when we thought your parents were making you move to New York City?" Hailee offered. "You ate so much cake, your stomach hurt for a week." She took a deep breath.

"I cried so hard, I threw up. Mom and Dad spent an hour reassuring me. To this day, the smell of yellow cake with white frosting makes me queasy."

She looked at me with a smile I knew she had to dig deep for. "Are you going to keep seeing him?" she asked. A silence stretched on, and neither of us knew what to do with it. This whole day felt different now, and it was nowhere near over.

I looked back down at my shoes and took a breath. I knew the next words out of my mouth were going to be a lie, but it was a lie that was going to save our friendship. I wasn't sure why Hailee was this upset, but I'd do anything to make it stop. Hailee kept looking at the door and away from me like she was planning an escape. I wanted out of this too.

"No," I lied, and pressed my sock-covered toe deeper into the floor. I hoped it was convincing. I used my firmest voice and shook my head as I said it. Hailee didn't respond. She pulled her hair back into a bun, looked at me briefly, and chewed on her lip, laughing a little to herself before picking up our tote bags and putting them in her room.

I turned on the TV and found the Hallmark Channel, hoping it would lighten the mood, but when Hailee returned to the living room, she still kept her distance. We both sighed in relief when Mama J opened the door. Desperate for a distraction, we sprang into action to help her with the bags. After washing our hands and making the food, the conversation flowed much more easily. Janice surprised us with sundaes and trips down memory lane. We made rings in the backyard as promised; Hailee even tagged me in a few pictures and commented about how beautiful the rings looked. Still, when we went to bed that night, things felt fractured.

"Best part of today?" I asked from where I lay on my back, looking at the ceiling. I wanted so badly to find some comfort in the five stars that remained, but I had to scoot closer to Hailee to see them, and that felt like something I shouldn't do. So, I waited with the silence keeping me company in the dark room. Hailee didn't answer at first. She lay on her side away from me. I felt myself crying again, and hoped Hailee could not hear the tears.

"I'm too tired to do this today," Hailee said, after a minute that felt like an hour. "Night, Drea."

"Okay, love you," I replied.

The silence came back again; Hailee had probably already fallen asleep, even though she had never missed saying it back before. I lay there wide awake with the quiet teasing me and my tears; it felt like even the streetlights outside were going home to their families. I was surprised to find that I was ready to go home too.

I slid out of the bed as quietly as I could the next morning and went to the bathroom. When I returned, I saw that Dad had texted.

> Daddy: Ready when you are, sweet pea.
> Andrea: Now is good.
> Daddy: Okay, see you in a few minutes.

I was grateful that Hailee was a heavy sleeper as I packed my suitcase and grabbed my tote bag. I wasn't in the mood to change out of my pajamas. I'd do that later. I put my suitcase in the living room and hugged Mama J, who was making herself coffee. I decided against waking Hailee to say goodbye. We would see each other on Friday for the amusement park anyway. I sat and talked with Janice until Dad texted that he was there. I hugged Janice again and she pulled back, but didn't let go.

"I don't know what is going on, but you two will be fine, I know that." Janice smiled and kissed me on the forehead. I wasn't so sure she was right this time. Once I was safely inside the car with my seat belt fastened, Dad pulled off.

I waited until we were in the living room before I opened the tote and pulled out the gift I had bought for him. We sat together on the couch as he opened it. Our positions were similar to the ones Hailee and I had been in on her couch yesterday. I had to try really hard not to think about what happened there.

Dad made quick work of the wrapping to find a baseball mitt. I am not a big baseball fan, but Dad is, and he talked constantly about the Yankees games Grandpa Sam took him to as a kid. When Grandpa Sam passed away last summer, just before my big surgery, Dad took it really hard. He was so busy making sure that I was good to go, he never took true time to grieve. Mom and I had spent so much time trying to figure out how to help him, but our every plan failed. He never said as much out loud, but I knew that when he stopped watching baseball on TV, it was because it had become too hard. When I saw the mitt at the art show, it hit me. Maybe this was the way to cheer up Daddy, who wore his grief on his sleeves closest to his heart.

"We could toss the ball around for a bit?" I offered, trying my best to seem nonchalant about it. The smile that spread across his face before he hug-tackled me into the couch was all the answer I needed. When we lifted ourselves back into a sitting position, Dad laughed and cleared his throat.

"Thank you, sweet pea. I'd like that," he said, standing up and walking to the kitchen. "I'm going to make you breakfast now." I watched as he tried and failed to slyly wipe his eyes before washing his hands. "It's dusty here today." I nodded back, but he laughed anyway.

I grabbed my tote bag and slung it back on my shoulder. I rubbed my right knee before standing. "Where's Mom?" I called out, walking around the couch. I watched Dad in the kitchen from where I stood. He always looked the most at peace when he was cooking. That was the thing we had in common: he loved cooking the way I loved art.

"Bedroom," he said. I watched him whisk the eggs a little bit and then left to find Mom. I walked back out to the foyer and down the hall, knocking twice before I pushed the door open to find her at the vanity. I sat on the bed and watched her with slight envy as she perfectly applied her eyeliner. Mom looked at me in the mirror and smiled. She set her makeup down and walked over to sit next to me.

"How was New York?" I asked, but I hugged her before I let her answer. A rush of emotions hit me.

"Good, but we missed you. Your bribes are already upstairs in the room you need to clean." She laughed at my responding groan. "How was Hailee's?" Mom pulled back to look at my face, and that's when I lost it. My bottom lip started to quiver. Mom moved us over to the ottoman without saying a word. She brushed the hair out of my face to find that my tears were fully falling now.

"It was kind of horrible, Mom. I lied to her and we fought and then we tried to be okay but I didn't say goodbye when I left and she . . ." I blubbered out. Mom got up to grab tissues, and when she sat back down, I took three and used them all at once.

"Oh sweetie. I'm so sorry," she said. I contemplated what I felt comfortable telling her. I didn't know how much of my broken heart to share just yet. I didn't think this was the right moment to come out, but was there ever a right moment?

"She didn't say 'I love you' back last night. I know that's silly, but—"

"No buts, you two are close. It's understandable that you're upset," Mom said. She wiped away my tears, but the ache in my chest just made me cry harder.

"She was upset because she thinks I ditched her for George, but it wasn't like I planned it," I sighed.

"Who is George?" Mom asked. I knew she was trying her best to keep up with my train of thought, but the line of questions wasn't really helping. She handed me more tissues. I blew my nose once more loudly.

"Mom, focus!" I demanded, but there was no real frustration behind it. I bit my lip and looked down at the elephants on my socks, wiggling my toes. At least they were happy. That must be nice.

"Honey, I'm trying," she said. She blew out a breath and smiled wearily at me.

"Anyway, tell me about New York," I insisted. I got up to wipe my face and pull my hair back in a messy bun, gathering the tissues too and throwing them in my parents' garbage. I stopped walking when I reached the vanity, taking four deep breaths before going back to Mom. She tapped my knee once I sat. I closed my eyes at the contact; it was the thing she had done since I was a kid, a reminder that she had my back no matter what. It always helped. I watched the way the sun slung around Mom's shoulders. I wanted freckles so bad, but no, I'd had to take after dad's freckle-free side.

"Well, New York was nice. The crisis we averted was someone trying to leak the fall collection online. It was not quite as do-or-die as Fredrick insinuated. We handled it and everything was fine, really—"

"That's what I thought about Hailee, but here we are. It's not like I was ditching the list, ya know?" I asked. I didn't mean to take over the conversation, but I couldn't help it. I sighed and started hiccupping from the crying. Once I got that under control, I took another deep breath and my loose bun fell out, which made me start crying again.

"Here, let me," Mom murmured, motioning. I said nothing as I turned to let her fix it. I debated telling her the next part.

"She asked me if I liked him and if I was going to see him again," I said, running my left hand over the back of my right one. Another nervous habit. I could still see the look on Hailee's face as she asked the question: like the answer determined something that neither of us fully understood. I didn't want to lose Hailee, and loving her wasn't an option either, so . . . I had lied. Maybe George could be just as lovable if I let him. I had to try.

"Do you? Are you?" Mom asked as she finished arranging the bun. I turned back to face her, but said nothing else.

I looked around the room and my eyes landed on the picture of me, my parents, Hailee, and Janice after Mom's fashion show in New York last year. Only our parents were looking at the camera as we all stood arm in arm. Hailee and I were gazing at each other with smiles so big, I could feel the excitement still. I remembered the butterflies and the rise of my chest when Hailee's and my eyes caught that day. I remembered the stir in my stomach every time we were close; how it scared and excited me even when I refused to name what it was. Looking at the picture now, I felt scared still: scared that I was going to lose my best friend either way.

"I don't know if I like him, but I want to try. He wants to hang out again, and if we do, I can't tell Hailee," I said finally. I let a silence fall over us and pulled Mom's gift out of my tote bag. A thing that the public did not know about Mom was that as much as she loved her career, she had always dreamed of living in a small town and raising a kid who was as normal as possible. Heartbreak aside, I thought I'd turned out alright, and I really liked to buy her little reminders of the other dream that came true for her. So, this time I bought her a little sign with our town's name on it.

"I love it and you so much," Mom said. I squeezed her tight, but I could tell there was something more she wanted to say. I raised an eyebrow.

"Come out with it. You're the one always reminding me that we Williams women mean what we say and say what we mean. I can take it," I stated. I stood to stretch quickly, and she helped me count.

As I gathered my things to leave, Mom took me up on it. "I just wonder if you should even be hanging out with someone you'd have to lie to Hailee about?" We walked out of the bedroom and down the hall. I could smell the bacon from here—at least one thing was certain, breakfast was going to be delicious.

"It's complicated, Mom," I said, before we reached the kitchen. I stopped and looked at my phone: nothing from Hailee. I hated how annoyed I was by her silence. I opened social media.

@DreaWArt: #BSEList continues Friday! See you then loves! @HaileeTxo @FiThatsMe @OhCharlie and @OliviaHope #ILoveRollerCoasters #OllyOlly

@OliviaHope: @DreaWArt @HaileeTxo @FiThatsMe
@OhCharlie You're the first pickup so be ready
on time! #OxenFree

I rolled my eyes but liked the post.

@FiThatsMe: @OliviaHope: @DreaWArt @HaileeTxo
@OhCharlie I can't wait to see Merv. He's driving
us, right? #CurlyFriesAndSlowRides
@OliviaHope: @DreaWArt @HaileeTxo @FiThatsMe
@OhCharlie Yes. I'll tell him you say hello.
@HaileeTxo: "@OliviaHope: @DreaWArt @OhCharlie
@FiThatsMe #MervOverEverything

I smiled at Hailee's post. Normally I'd text her and
agree, but maybe Hailee needed some space from me for a
few days. I could give her that. My phone was down for only
a few moments before I got a text alert. I wanted it to be
Hailee, but when I picked the phone, I smiled anyway.

G: Roller Coasters huh?
Andrea: Hi George. Yes. I love them!
G: The boys and I will be there too. Jamie is going
to be so happy to see you
Andrea: ♥
G: So, will you ride a few coasters with me?

Andrea: Yeah, throw in some ice cream and you
have a deal!

G: Done. I'll text you when we get there to see when
you can sneak away.

Andrea: Ha! Fiona is distracted by curly fries, Charlie
loves the water park, Jamie will probably distract
Olivia.

G: So, Hailee is my main competition? Got it.

Andrea: I wouldn't say that.

G: See you there beautiful.


I took a few minutes and turned the word *beautiful* over in my head a few times. No one outside of my family and friends had ever called me beautiful before. I didn't know what to do with that information, so I did what anyone in my situation would do . . . I ignored it.


Andrea: See you!

I waved goodbye to my parents after reassuring them that I had my portable charger, Tiger Balm, extra sunscreen, and sunglasses in my backpack. True to her word, Olivia was on time and made a point to greet my parents with hugs and polite conversation. Seeing them together brought me back too much, and, uncomfortable, I excused myself from the conversation. Merv leaned up against the car door and smiled at me.

"Good seeing you, Miss Andrea," he said as I approached. Merv had been Olivia's driver since Olivia and I were kids. Olivia was still too scared to drive outside of Gardenia, so Merv drove every time we left it. He and I had bonded immediately over being Black and disabled. Merv used a hearing aid in his left ear, and though our disabilities weren't the same, Merv made me feel understood and less alone in a way that my parents and friends (save Faye and Vanessa) could not.

"Merv! Hi. How's James and Merv Jr.?" I asked, and beamed at his hearty laugh. We hugged and I leaned against the car beside him. I followed a passing car as it moved behind each tree by my house.

"My husband and son—*Andrew*—are good. Thank you for asking," Merv replied. He waved at my parents and checked his watch.

"I'm glad to hear it. Hug them for me?" I asked. I looked at my watch and groaned, then shouted, "Olivia, let's go! You'll see them tomorrow at the anniversary dinner." Olivia turned around and rolled her eyes, but said goodbye.

"Will do. I've also been asked to tell you that the reason you keep losing to Andrew in rummy is because you refuse to call him anything but Merv Jr. Though that makes no sense," Merv added. I let out a howl of a laugh as he opened up the door for me to slide in.

"It's superstition and teenage silliness, but you two should've made him a Jr. just for fun," I said as he shut the door.

"Not our style." Merv answered, climbing into the driver's seat as Olivia rounded the car to the passenger side. I put on my seat belt. I pulled a pack of gum out of my backpack and offered it to the car as she got in. Merv declined, but Olivia grabbed a piece and said nothing, and otherwise acted like she was too good to speak to me unless forced. I could do the same—I wasn't above being petty back. The only sound from my house to Hailee's was that of the radio.

When I saw Hailee, I sucked in a breath. She was beautiful as ever, her black hair in a high ponytail. She wore a dusty pink eyeshadow that I loved and which paired well with her plain white shirt and white Keds.

"Hey," I said when she slid in next to me in the back seat. I tried my best to smile normally, but I was nervous, so it probably looked like I was wincing a little. I watched Hailee fasten her seat belt.

"Hey," Hailee said back. She said something to Olivia that I only half heard over my own thoughts. Hailee remained with her eyes forward, talking to Olivia, who was suddenly full of conversation. A quick look downwards told me that Hailee was rubbing her thumb and index finger together, something she only did when she was nervous. I was relieved to know I was not the only one.

"Hails, your jean shorts are so cute," I said. Hailee smiled at me and it felt like I could breathe again. I rolled down my window to let some air in and put on my sunglasses. After we sang the chorus to the song on the radio, Hailee responded.

"Thanks, A. Can we be good again? I missed you." She held out her hand palm up. I smiled and took it. I squeezed her hand and nodded.

"Cheese and pep, pep and cheese."

We hugged and Olivia clapped. We pulled apart and laughed.

"Didn't even know Andrea was annoying you, Hail, but I'm glad she won't have to spend the day staring at you with those sad eyes." Olivia chuckled at herself. I left it alone, because she wasn't wrong. Merv pulled into Fiona and Charlie's driveway and beeped twice. Charlie appeared first, her signature Converses in blue today, paired with black cut-off shorts that I was sure belonged to Fiona and a shirt that almost perfectly matched her sneakers. Fiona was not far behind, wearing red shorts, a white and red shirt, and flip-flops, her hair in a loose braid.

～～～

I hated cotton candy but I ate it anyway. I smiled for pictures and took a bunch of my own. We rode as many roller coasters as I could convince the group to. We went to the water park, and Charlie decided she never wanted to leave the water again while Hailee and I stuck to the rides. We walked back to the others with our arms linked. Everything was really starting to feel okay again.

"That last one was the best one," Hailee decided.

We strolled past a wall decorated with waves, perfect for a picture, so we doubled back and asked a nice, older woman named Heather to take our picture. We took a normal one, and then Hailee surprised me by wrapping her arms around my waist and kissing me on the cheek. I couldn't help the wide smile I gave in return as the final picture was taken. I thanked the woman and Hailee grabbed her phone.

"You two are so cute together. Have a great day," Heather said. I stammered a clarification while Hailee nodded.

"Thank you," Hailee added on, beaming at Heather, who nodded her head once more before leaving us. "That was nice." Hailee bounced on her heels, her energy contagious. She ate the last of my cotton candy and jogged around me in a circle. She stopped and lifted her face up to the sky as people moved around us. After a few more moments, we linked arms again and began walking toward the meetup spot. The sun came out in full force as we moved. It was the kind of sticky hot that I complained about now, but missed so much during the winter months. I contain multitudes.

Hailee squeezed my arm as she held it. This always let me know that it was okay to put some more of my weight on her when my leg was hurting. Sure, it had taken years of understanding, but I loved that I never had to say it out loud. Hailee just knew when I needed the help. I tapped the inside of Hailee's right arm twice. Thank you.

We reached the meeting point to find Charlie pouting and Fiona and Olivia in a spirited discussion about the best Disney Princess. As we blended with the group, Hailee let go of my hand and cleared her throat, like we had almost been caught doing something wrong. I said nothing about it, but felt the sting anyway. After we all agreed that Sleeping Beauty was the worst princess, my phone vibrated.

G: Ice cream?
Andrea: Be there in ten.

"Hey, I know we are going to do the swings next, but I think I'm going to go grab some ice cream and rest my legs," I said, putting my phone away.

To my surprise, I heard Olivia speak up immediately. "I'll go with her," she announced. All of our eyes turned to her, and Olivia squirmed under the weight of our gazes. "What? I just want some ice cream," she shrugged.

"We'll meet back up after the swings? Right, Olivia?" I asked. Olivia hummed noncommittally, but I knew she agreed. Hailee smiled at me and gave me a thumbs-up before we parted. It was cute that Hailee thought Olivia and I would come out of ice cream in a better place, so I just smiled back.

When Olivia and I were out of earshot, Olivia spoke: "I am onto you. Sneaking to go see George and lying to your best friend about it?"

"What are you talking about?" I feigned ignorance. Olivia scoffed and I knew I was caught.

"You insult me. I saw you two hugging at the art show: Lacey sent the picture to me, Fi, and Charlie. What I *am* curious about though is why you're keeping it from Hailee." She flicked her wrist as though she didn't care if I answered her or not, but kept her eyes on me.

"Because I'm in love with Hailee and she'll never feel the same," I blurted out. My face was hot from the admission; my breath caught in my throat. We both froze like we were kids again, playing Simon Says, until Olivia reached for me and then thought better of it, pulling her hand back quickly.

"Andrea, I know you're in love with her. But why are you keeping George from her?" Olivia asked, her tone accusatory.

"What—what are you talking about?" I asked. Olivia fixed me with a *girl, please* look.

"I know you, and honestly, it's obvious," she started. My eyes bugged out involuntarily, which must have startled her because she spoke again quickly. "Not to Hails, though . . . I don't think she has any idea."

"Yeah?" I asked, hopeful. "Olivia, if she knew, I'd lose her. There's no way that she feels the same. I already know what it is like to lose someone I was close to. I don't want to do that again." Olivia began looking at me cautiously. She cleared her throat a few times like she did when we were kids and she had needed time to gather her thoughts before speaking again. I watched her for a few more moments, strangely soothed by it, despite my racing heart.

Finally, she asked quietly, "How do you know she'll never feel the same?" She kept her distance but made sure only I could hear. The question snapped me out of my daze.

I began walking again, faster than before. Olivia caught up easily. We went in silence for a few moments. I paid attention to literally anyone else, like the couple making out against the wall at the end of the bathroom line, the brothers fighting in the Ferris wheel line, the bored roller-coaster operator texting on his phone after starting the ride. When I finally looked over at Olivia, I saw that she still looked nervous. Olivia was never nervous.

"Why did you jump to come with me now?" I asked. I was sure the answer was not just ice cream—or Hailee.

"Jamie texted he's with George. He never texts me first." Olivia shrugged, but I did not miss the vulnerability in her eyes. I was struck by how much she seemed to like Jamie. There was a part of me that wondered, when she started, what did she like about him most? But I couldn't ask. It was no longer my place to.

"Don't look at me like that. We are not talking about it, and we are not friends."

"Okay, but maybe you shouldn't be with someone that makes you do all the work," I said.

"It's not like that," Olivia replied. "You wouldn't get it."

"If you say so," I answered as we rounded the corner and George and Jamie came into view. They both stood up from the bench when they saw us.

"You look beautiful, ladies," George said, though he never took his eyes off me. He was a little heavy-handed, but

I would allow it. I smiled at him and ducked my head under his gaze.

"Laying it on a little thick," Olivia said, coming to stand beside me.

"He's right though," Jamie agreed, looking only at Olivia. It was Olivia's turn to look bashful.

"Oh," Olivia managed. Jamie smiled at her and took her hand; they walked over to the line first. George came over to me and we hugged.

"You look great too," I said when we stepped out of the hug. His eyes were still the perfect shade of green and his hair was perfectly styled. He wore a red, short-sleeved shirt, and I let myself enjoy his toned arms, courtesy of soccer. Toned arms that I knew matched a pack of abs I had gotten a peek at during a game. We held hands while we walked over to join Olivia and Jamie. I tried my best not to note the differences between his hand and Hailee's.

I ordered two scoops of butter pecan ice cream; Olivia ordered mint chocolate chip; Jamie, plain vanilla; and George, a chocolate-and-vanilla swirl. We laughed and talked, and despite knowing the truth, it felt a little like Olivia and I were real friends again and I did not hate it. As quick as the thought came, though, I pushed it away.

"We have to go," Olivia said after a while, looking at her phone. I sighed but stood. George kissed my hand. Olivia and Jamie rolled their eyes but then shared a moment of their own.

THE SECRET SUMMER PROMISE

"Come to Andrea's parents' anniversary thing tomorrow?" Olivia asked. Jamie and George looked at me for confirmation. At first I wanted to kill Olivia for making the invite, but after thinking about it for a second, I wasn't really opposed. Hailee had said she had to leave early—if they came at the end, she'd be gone and would never have to know.

"Yeah, sure, you can come toward the end. I'll text you the details," I answered. Jamie smiled in thanks and George mouthed, *Can't wait*! with a wink.

"Bye!" Olivia said before pulling me forward. When we passed the Ferris wheel, she let go of my arm. "I know, I know. I owe you big."

"You do."

~~~

When Olivia and I met back up with the rest of the group, Hailee was the first to speak. "Did you guys know that George and Jamie are here?" she asked. Olivia and I looked at each other quickly. Olivia pushed her sunglasses from her forehead back down over her eyes.

"No," I said. I looked at each of the girls before standing beside Hailee again.

"We just grabbed the ice cream," Olivia added. "The line was ridiculous. I spent forever listening to this one drone about how great summer is while she rested her legs." I rolled my eyes, but quickly nodded at Olivia and hoped she understood the *thank you* within it.

"And Olivia spent forever trying to convince me that winter was superior while she basked in the sun, so . . ." I trailed off as Olivia crossed her arms with a huff. I hoped the girls were buying this.

"Glad you two are making progress," Fiona said sarcastically. She placed both hands on her hips and steadied us with her most authoritative glare. I tried not to laugh behind my hand. "But we are *not* leaving here without my curly fries. I have suffered long enough!"

Hailee chuckled and grabbed Fiona's arm. Charlie took Hailee's and they were off. Olivia and I hung behind but stayed close enough not to draw suspicion. I bit the inside of my cheek. This was going to be awkward—there was no other way around it.

In all honesty, I still was a little stunned that Olivia had lied for me just now. I had spent too long thinking that—given the opportunity—Olivia would throw me under the bus just because she could. When we were kids, Olivia was a stickler for the truth: she told my parents everything, and was always so eager for their approval, even if that meant admitting how the watercolors got on the living room carpet, or that time we snuck down the stairs in the middle of the night and ate so much ice cream, we made ourselves sick in the morning. Now, Olivia was lying by choice, for me: her sworn enemy. And I was grateful, even if I could not help the pang of guilt behind it.

"Thank you," I eventually said, quietly. Olivia stared at me for a long moment before shaking her head. We walked once more in silence, and for a second, I wasn't sure if she'd actually heard me. I opened my mouth to say it again, but Olivia interrupted me.

"Debt paid. But let's still stay out of each other's way. Okay?" She stopped walking, her hands on her hips. I remembered when she'd leveled that look at Gigi Kessler in the fourth grade, when Gigi had made fun of the way I walked at recess. Gigi had cried and ran to find a teacher, but I was so grateful that I declared we'd be best friends forever, shortly after.

Olivia and I were much older now, but being on the receiving end of that look stung me more than I was ever willing to admit. She left me there, jogging a bit to catch up with the others. I kept my original pace and blew out a breath. I used the moment alone to organize my thoughts. I was going to keep seeing George because I liked the way he made me feel. The love might come later—after all, we'd only hung out twice. All I had to do was keep lying a little to my best friend. Once we reached the curly-fry line, Hailee fell back from the others to join me.

"Let's split a large one?" she asked. I nodded. Hailee grabbed my arm and smiled. "Lean against me."

I did as I was told, and it was then that my brain caught up to the rest of my body. I was exhausted. When it was Hailee's turn to order, Charlie and Fiona took my arms from either side and smiled at me too. We were like a well-oiled machine. They helped without me having to ask.

"Love you so much," I said, my voice breaking a little. Hailee grabbed the curly fries for us and Olivia held a container in each hand. One had to be Fiona's. When we made it back to Merv, I climbed in the car and sighed in relief. Hailee climbed in beside me, Fiona following her, and then Olivia, letting Charlie take the passenger seat.

"How was it, ladies?" Merv asked, starting the car and pulling out of the parking lot. Fiona grabbed her fries from Olivia and looked at them adoringly.

"Olly Olly," Olivia chanted. She smiled at everyone, her phone in her hand.

"Oxen Free!" we joined in.

"That good, huh?" Merv laughed, and turned on the radio. Everyone went back to regular conversation. Fiona sang songs loudly in between bites of curly fries, Hailee joined her on the choruses, Merv and Charlie talked about jazz of all things, and Olivia smiled down at her phone. I pulled my own out to send a sappy post and take a picture for Instagram, and then I saw the text alert.

Olivia: Jamie asked me out on a date!
Andrea: That's great! Omg!

Olivia didn't respond, but I watched the smile on her face shift to muted amazement as she put her phone down. I decided to corral everyone in for a picture. We squeezed in like sardines just to make sure we were all there, and Charlie basically contorted her body so she could be too. Merv opted out because he was driving. I made him promise that he would partake next time before Hailee chanted, "Merv Over Everything!" and everyone giggled.

Once we were satisfied with the set of pictures, I texted them to the group and opened up my Instagram.

> @DreaWArt: Amusement Park fun. With friends like these, I get to be my best self. I love you all so much #BSEList #MyBestFriendsDoItBetter ❤☺

"I'm excited to put on a really nice dress and celebrate with your parents tonight," Hailee singsonged. I clapped for her like an appreciative audience should. Uncrossing her legs and pretending to bow despite the fact that we were in lawn chairs, Hailee beamed over at me.

"Same! It should be a lot of fun," I replied with a smile of my own. Tonight was going to be great, I knew it. I ran my hands down my legs and looked up toward the sky; the clouds shaped like tea kettles made me laugh.

We lay across the lounge chairs, and though the backyard was fenced in, we could hear cars as they passed. I had always been fascinated by the idea of where these nameless and faceless people were going. Did they long for more like me? Or were they completely content? Did they know who to love or how to? I knew I had time to figure it out, but I wasn't sure how much time I actually had.

I loved portraits for that very reason: they captured people where they were—which created magical moments for them, sure—but painting people was also about the way I saw them. I think that's why the idea of getting out into the world and meeting those nameless and faceless people excited me so much. I could capture them the way they hoped while giving them a glimpse into how I saw them. I couldn't wait. My phone vibrated and I snuck a glance at Hailee, who started playing music on her phone immediately after. She sang along, but remained looking forward.

> G: I have been thinking . . . Why am I always the
> one to text first?
> Andrea: Are you? I guess I never really thought
> about it.
> G: I'm sad about it. How will you make it up to me?
> Andrea: Why am I always having to make something
> up to you?
> G: Keeps you on your toes. I want to see you, what
> are you doing?
> Andrea: You'll see me later, remember?
> G: Yes, but since you're only hoping I'll pop by after
> Hailee leaves . . .
> Andrea: That's not true!
> G: It is. But you're cute so I'll let it slide.

Andrea: Thank you.

G: So, a week from Tuesday? Let me take you out to
eat.

G: 7:30?

Andrea: 5:30 I'm hungry way earlier than 7:30

G: 5:30 it is.


"Who are you texting?" Hailee asked. I jumped at the question and dropped my phone. I scrambled to pick it up. Hailee watched me from where she sat; by the time the song on her phone changed, I was back in the chair with my phone.

"Sorry, you scared me. Charlie. She was asking if Mom was ever going to start making sneakers," I said. I was concerned about how much easier the lying was getting. Hailee bought it, though, because she said nothing else.

"It's too bad that you're still so jumpy after all these years," she teased. She got up from the lounge chair and walked out into the grass.


Andrea: Gotta go.


I put my phone on the table beside me and didn't move.

"Remember how we used to play out here for hours? And the day we decided to buy houses next door to each other when we were older?" Hailee asked, turning around. I watched her spin in a circle, her face to the sky and her hands up in the air. The sun called me, so I got up to join her. We spun more, our laughter filling the air. We eventually fell to the ground like we did when we were kids, bright-eyed and eager. I'd pay for it later, but right now, I didn't care.

"Mine was going to be pink and yours blue," I laughed. We moved to sit across from each other cross-legged. I smiled as the sun beamed down on me, like it was happy too, or like it was working to restore my body so that my pain would not be so bad later. A bit of a stretch, sure. Either way, I was always thankful for it.

"Our husbands would be best friends, just like us. We'd have babies from kissing," Hailee added, and we laughed at our younger selves. I watched Hailee's face fall slightly for a moment. She tapped her hands on her knees but said nothing.

"What's up?" I asked. I smiled at her encouragingly, then scrunched my nose in an effort to make her laugh. She did not.

"I guess I just don't know if I am excited to get older anymore. There are so many scary things about being an adult that I don't want to face alone," Hailee said.

"You won't face it alone. You'll have your husband and your blue house," I joked. I wasn't sure how to handle this change in conversation. I stretched out my legs, but tilted my body away so that they weren't touching Hailee.

"I'm serious . . . what if I no longer want a blue house or a husband?" Hailee asked, uncrossing her own legs but fixing me with a stare.

"Well, what do you want instead?" I asked in a whisper. I picked the grass with my left hand and rubbed it with my thumb and pointer finger. I didn't know what to do in this conversation. Hailee placed her hands flat on the grass and sighed. She looked at me like I should know what she was thinking, but I was all out of ideas. This wasn't like us, and the thought of that made me queasy. Hailee tried again, her right brow furrowed as she closed her eyes, breathing in through her nose and out through her mouth. She turned toward me, resolved to say whatever was on her mind.

"I don't think I can have what I want. Can I?" Hailee asked, her voice unsure. She began plucking blades of glass too. At least there was something we could share in this moment.

"I can't answer that for you, but . . . I think you deserve whatever you want," I decided.

"I don't want to get attached to anyone I might lose," Hailee said simply. She looked away from me and toward the patio door. The sun was leaving and night was starting to cast through the trees. But the stars weren't ready yet.

"I don't think that's how it works," I replied, after a moment. "Love or attachment isn't something you can avoid. It's not that easy."

I watched Hailee stand and brush grass blades off her legs. "Well, it should be," she said, still looking at the patio door. I stood too, letting silence hang between us.

"You girls can only be out there for a few more minutes!" my mom called out through the door. "We have to start setting up soon, and you two need to change."

"Okay, coming!" we said in unison.

We walked toward the house, but not before I grabbed my phone. The weirdness from our conversation lingered inside me; I figured that Hailee was still upset in some way. The trouble was that I couldn't figure out why or how to fix it—but her not wanting to get too attached to someone she could lose stung in a way I couldn't pinpoint entirely.

~~~

The party was in full swing, the backyard beautifully decorated with twinkling lights, blue handcrafted centerpieces, and a crowd of our close family and friends at assigned tables. Everyone was looking at my parents, me, Hailee, Olivia, and Janice—our "immediate family table," as mom called it while on the phone with Denise, the event planner. Fredrick, Uncle D and Faye and Venessa sent their regrets. Fredrick was spending the weekend with their mom, who was visiting the city. Uncle D was also in the city—I didn't know why though. And Faye and Vanessa's parents couldn't justify making the drive across the state for the night. They sent their love. The night was beginning to look a lot like a wedding reception, which made me smile.

The string quartet was softly playing in the corner as my parents stared lovingly at each other. We had already made the rounds as instructed. We'd said hello and thank you to everyone for coming, though Hailee, Olivia, and I spent most of our time at Charlie and Fiona's table and let Mom, Dad, and Janice do the heavy lifting. Mama J didn't mind it, though— she sold some jewelry in the process. A fact we would force her to celebrate when we had the time. For now, we were back at our table, full after having seconds, and ready to dance. But first, the speeches.

"You got this," Hailee whispered as I stood and tapped my glass. Light reflected off of my ruby-red dress. I smiled as I waited for everyone to turn their attention to me. The string quartet stopped playing; Fi gave me one exaggerated wink to make me laugh.

"Hello everyone. First, I want to say thank you all for coming out tonight to celebrate these two crazy kids. If you didn't know, I'm their daughter Andrea."

"They know . . . I don't shut up about you at work," Dad cut in. This led to laughter and some applause.

"For the record, I don't either," Mom added. She leaned into Dad's chest and the crowd laughed and applauded again.

"Anyway, as their daughter—" I paused to look back over at my parents, who gave me the thumbs-up to keep going. "As their daughter, I get to see their love firsthand every day, and it really is as special as it seems. Don't get me wrong, it can be gross at times—I am, after all, a seventeen-year-old who doesn't need to see them kiss every morning." I joined the crowd in their laughter. "But the kind of love they have is the kind of love I hope to have. A love that is patient, constant, and worth the work. I'll leave you with my gift—" I nodded at our neighbor Garret to pull the covering off the painting to the right of us. When he did, everyone gasped. It felt good. I turned to my parents and raised my glass of iced tea. "To Evelyn and Derek."

"Aht. Aht." Dad called before Mom playfully slapped his shoulder. I shook my head fondly.

"To Mom and Dad," I corrected. I watched them for a moment, one part of their bodies always touching as the crowd repeated the first toast. Their free hands were holding each other's. Mom turned back to me and mouthed, *I love you.* I mouthed it back before sitting down. Hailee beamed at me. My phone buzzed from the pocket of my dress, but I ignored it.

"You going to get that?" Olivia asked, looking down at my buzzing pocket and then pointedly back at me. I didn't have time for her question as my dad began his speech. The buzzing stopped, but then started again.

"Yes, after the speeches," I replied, turning my attention back to my dad, and then my mom when she took over for him. The applause was loud as they finished, and soon the string quartet carried off their instruments and the DJ made quick work of setting up his station. He began playing all of the oldies first, so my parents, Janice, and the other older partygoers got up to dance. Fiona and Charlie came and took their seats and we talked for a bit.

"Oh my gosh, it's our song!" Charlie said. She grabbed a reluctant Olivia out of her seat. Fiona grabbed Hailee who grabbed me as the first verse of "Pretty Girl Rock" hit.

We ran to the middle of the floor and Fiona shouted, "My name is Keri!" Hailee sang the next lines, I sang the one that followed, and we all turned to Olivia, who sighed, but shouted the last two. We all joined in for the rest and through the chorus, then danced and sang to the songs that followed.

"God bless Mama Williams' Empowerment Playlist," Charlie stated to a circle of nods in agreement about twenty minutes later. "I'm going to get a drink, y'all coming?" Before I could answer, Olivia cut in.

"Drea and I are good," she offered. She grabbed my arm and pulled me aside while the others shrugged and left the floor.

"What gives?" I asked. "You said we should go back to hating each other, remember?"

"Worry not, I still hate you, but . . . since you don't look at your texts sent to warn you that they are on their way . . ."

"Oh my God. He's here. Right now," I said. I watched George walking up to the party from across our lawn. He wore black slacks and a black button down shirt that hugged his arms. He looked good. He waved sheepishly as he and Jamie began walking toward me and Olivia.

"Yes, and so is the best friend you promised you'd stop seeing him," Olivia said flatly. Out of the corner of my eye I saw the girls returning with their drinks. Hailee held two, likely one for me, and my stomach dropped. I turned back to Olivia in a panic. They were all going to reach us at the same time. The dance floor was nearly empty now.

"Hey Jamie, hey George," Fiona said. She looked back and forth between me and Hailee as she said George's name.

"It's really good to see you, Olivia," Jamie said. They smiled at each other, and Charlie cleared her throat.

"Of course, it's great to see all of you," he clarified. We shook our heads, but no one believed him. Hailee refused to look at me, but I watched her down both drinks.

"Hey, great to see all of you, how's your summer?" George asked. He winked at me like he was scoring brownie points. The wink did nothing to help my knotted stomach.

"Same old, same old," Charlie supplied. To his credit, George nodded like she'd told him the most interesting story.

"Thanks for coming, you two," Olivia said, but she only looked at Jamie. The DJ started playing slow songs, so we moved to the side and out of the way.

"Thanks for inviting us, but we can only stay for a second. He's got practice in the morning, and I drove," Jamie shrugged. "We wanted to say hi though."

"Already?" Olivia asked. She ignored everyone's looks. She had it bad. Enemy aside, it was nice to see.

"Yeah, but I'll see this one a week from Tuesday," George said. I stopped breathing even as I returned his smile.

"Tuesday?" Hailee asked. Tuesday. The first word she'd said this entire time, and still she wouldn't look at me.

"This one agreed to let me take her on a date. You don't mind if I take her off your hands, do you?" George leaned in like he was telling Hailee a juicy secret. She smiled at him, and to the untrained eye, she seemed fine. She laughed like it was funny, placing her left hand on her chest as she did so, slapping his right arm playfully to sweeten the deal.

"She's all yours, it seems," Hailee replied, and said goodbye to them both. When they were gone, she excused herself, leaving Fiona, Charlie, Olivia, and me at a loss for words. None of them would look at me, though we all stood in a semi-circle, trying to process what had just happened.

"Well, that was—" Charlie began. Her eyes darted to the left to look at her sister, her hands on her hips, her shock palpable as she clasped and unclasped her hands.

"DEFCON bad," Fiona finished, rocking back and forth on her heels. The movement made me anxious, but I didn't ask her to stop. Fiona looked to Olivia like she could have the answer to fixing this, so I did too.

"What is DEFCON?" Olivia asked, no answer in sight. She started looking at me with an even mix of disappointment and pity.

"I don't actually know. I heard someone say it on TV once. Either way, Andrea, you should go find her," Fiona said.

I ran off the dance floor and into my parents, dancing off to the side of it with each other.

"Sweet pea, we love your gift. It's perfect," Mom said, before she spun and dipped me.

"I'm glad you guys liked it," I said, searching for Hailee as Dad took over, spinning me around in a circle. My mind was moving a mile a minute. I'd fucked up bad; my lie had caught up with me so fast I couldn't spin a new one, and now I was pretty sure I'd just lost my best friend. I couldn't stop the tears forming. I spotted Mama J off in the corner and she began walking toward us. She was crestfallen.

"Hi sweetie, she's in your bedroom," she said when she was within earshot.

"Honey, what's going on?" Mom asked, but I was already moving through the crowd.

"I'll explain later," I shouted back. I moved faster than I ever had to get to the house. Once I was inside, I made a mad dash to my bedroom. When I got there, Hailee was on my bed, her back to me. I walked in slowly, trying to assess the damage.

"Hails, I—"

"You know what's funny?" Hailee asked, looking out of the window, her back to me and the light from the open door casting itself onto her curled, black hair. Her hands clenched at her side. I could hear the tears in her voice. She laughed, but there was no humor in it. She turned around to face me. I moved toward her, and she recoiled, but continued: "What's funny is that I knew you were lying. That day at my house, when I asked you if you were going to keep seeing him? I knew you were lying," she accused, with a pointed finger.

"I can explain," I tried. I stopped walking, to give her space, but she stood and went across the room to my pink chair. I could see her running mascara after I turned on the light in the room. I shut my bedroom door for something to do. Hailee laughed again and it felt like a punch to the stomach.

"So do it. Explain," she said. Silence fell as she crossed her arms and waited. I tried to find the words to say, *I lied to keep you because if I told you the truth, you'd leave me.* Instead, I opened and closed my mouth a few times. All I managed was, "I'm sorry."

"I knew you couldn't. I'll tell you what . . . I'm sorry too. I'm sorry that I am sitting here crying over you. What I most regret though? The fact that I gave you the benefit of the doubt. If you can't explain, maybe I can help you."

"Hailee, please, I just–" I tried, reaching for her, searching for a moment to sort this out together and avoid what was coming. But she bulldozed past my words like I'd said nothing at all.

"So, it started during what was supposed to be our day at the art show. Ours. We get there, and you need space from me, and George Fallon just happens to be there?" she asked. I closed my eyes and reopened them.

"Yes."

"Bullshit. Not only do I not believe you, but why lie about it? Why couldn't you tell the person who is supposed to be your best friend the truth?" she demanded. I walked over to the bed and sat. I turned to face her.

"I knew that you were upset that I was late, and it just felt like you needed me to say no about George because you were annoyed that we'd spent the day apart."

"This isn't about you being late! It's about you being a liar!" Hailee yelled. She walked toward me and I felt my own anger begin to rise. She had no idea how hard it had been to maintain our friendship, when I had to do the quiet work of falling out of love at the same time.

"I lied to keep you!" I shouted back. Hailee's anger stole across her face; her mouth turned down as she gritted her teeth at me. We stood firmly in front of each other. Tears fell, but we didn't acknowledge them. I balled my fists and exhaled.

"You lied to keep me? That makes no sense. I was born at night, not *last night*, Andrea. You lied to protect yourself." Hailee closed the distance between us with every word. She leveled me with a glare before she wiped her tears.

"To protect my heart," I clarified. My yell quieted, but we both felt the heat of it. We were close enough now to feel each other's breaths.

"Yeah, well, either way you broke mine," Hailee choked out. Silence fell again. We could hear the party still in full swing through the window. At least everyone else was having a better time than us.

"I just want someone to want me. Why don't you want me to have that?" I asked, biting the inside of my cheek. Hailee's breath hitched. And then, in a whisper: "Tell me what he has that I don't."

"What?" I asked. Even though I'd heard her. My heart began to race, the rest of the miniscule distance between us closing.

"Is he funnier than me? Smarter than me? Do you melt when he smiles at you? Because you melt when I do. You laugh the hardest at my jokes, and I helped you pass math this year. So, what is it about him, or is it that he *is* a him?"

I couldn't respond. I couldn't breathe. She cupped my face and waited. I nodded eagerly as she wiped the few tears that remained. When our lips met, time stopped, and I felt like I was flying. I deepened the kiss; my hand found the small of her back. I was too excited to second-guess my decision.

Maybe we could have it all, friendship and love. We could grow old together, taking turns reading to each other on our future back porch. James and Jasmine, the twins we'd adopt, would come home from college and pretend to be annoyed by our doting. I was getting ahead of myself, so I left the future and turned my focus back to the lips on mine. This had become the best day ever and nothing was going to bring me down. Everything was perfect.

Until we needed air. Hailee gasped and pulled away.

"That was a mistake. God, I'm sorry," she said, pulling her mouth from mine, her face contorted like I had slapped her. She turned away from me, her body shivering like she'd been splashed with cold water, and then raced out of the room without looking back. I stood there, mouth open, tears streaming down my face once more. I touched my lips and closed my eyes.

How did my world begin and end in a single moment?

I woke up to my phone incessantly ringing. I guess I forgot to turn off the ringer. I thought of swiping it off of my nightstand in protest but stopped myself at the last second.

"Hello," I said groggily, trying and failing to wipe the sleep from my eyes.

"Are you still sleeping?" the other voice asked. The sun poured through my window as I swung my legs to the ground and reached for my glass of water.

"Yes, Olivia. Why wouldn't I be?" I asked incredulously. My heart was broken into a million little pieces. I had spent most of the night crying. What did she want from me?

"You have forty-five minutes to get ready. We are supposed to be at Randy's Paintball in like an hour. You forgot, didn't you?" Olivia stated. I ran a hand through my hair and walked toward my closet. I pulled out a pair of jean shorts and a T-shirt with purple stars on it.

"Can we not do this today? I barely slept last night and my head hurts from all the crying," I said hoarsely into the phone, then put it on speaker and tossed it on the bed. I turned toward my dresser and took a steadying breath. Olivia was silent on her end, at least until after I grabbed socks and underwear and walked back over to my bed.

"You were crying? Why, were you forced to let someone else take the spotlight for once?" she asked, chuckling at her own retort. I took a deep breath and felt the tears fighting their way to the wedges of my eyes. I put the clothes back down on the bed and grabbed the phone, taking it off speaker.

"Olivia, please," I begged. "I do not have it in me to go through this with you right now. Hailee kissed me and said it was a mistake, literally hours ago. Can you wait at least a week?" I whispered, rubbing my temple.

"Oh," Olivia said simply. Neither of us said anything for a while, the sounds of our breathing keeping time. "Well, Hailee will be there today. She already asked me to come get you. So maybe you can talk when we get there?" Olivia cleared her throat.

"Maybe," I supplied, though I wasn't hopeful.

"I'll be there in forty-two minutes," Olivia replied, hanging up the phone before I could say goodbye.

~~~

"Have you been to Randy's before?" Randy asked the six of us without a hint of irony. Charlie was the only one who shook her head yes. Randy laughed like he was in on a joke we weren't and continued on. "Split up into teams of three each, which is perfect because there are six of you here. Did you plan that?"

"Yep," Fiona said proudly, while Merv Jr. encouraged her to take a bow. She did. Merv Jr. was the one to decide who went on which team, since he was the most impartial. He stuck me and Olivia on the same team. I was hoping that Hailee was going to join us, just to defuse any tension. After all, she was usually the defuser between me and Olivia when we were at our worst. This time though, she stepped up and asked to be on the other team before Merv Jr. even named our last person. I tried to sew that wound with anger.

"Put on the gear that we've provided and head on out there. I've already given you a tour of the course. Have fun!" Randy said, stepping aside so we could grab the gear. Fiona helped me when I needed it, while Hailee pulled her hair back into a slick ponytail and I tried to ignore the way my breath hitched even as she pretended I wasn't there. I bit my lip and cleared my throat as we went off with our teams to either side of the course. Charlie, Merv Jr., and Hailee on one; me, Fiona, and Olivia on the other.

I had to get my head in the game and focus on winning; it was likely going to be the only joy I'd experience today. After crafting a quick plan of attack, my team was on the move. Fiona very dramatically did a tuck and roll to make it behind a rock that was only a few feet away. We all laughed as quietly as we could. Twenty minutes and a few close calls in, Merv Jr. took out Fiona, but then he stood there and let Olivia shoot him. After that, he and Fiona walked off the course together, arms looped and chatting a mile a minute. So it was just me, Olivia, Hailee, and Charlie left. We circled around each other for five minutes more of a stalemate before Olivia pulled me to the side.

"Listen, Charlie is almost too good at this," Olivia said, blowing a puff of hair out of her own face. I wasn't surprised: Charlie had great hand-eye coordination and 20/10 vision. It was annoying.

"I know! Do you have a plan?" I asked expectantly. Olivia always had a plan—it was sort of her thing. She had been the planner of the friend group for as long as any of us could remember. Sure, she was often the first person to bail at the end, but still.

"I can take her out if I go for her leg that's sticking out, but I'll have to die to do it. So you'll be on your own," Olivia said, like the hero in an action movie just before they sacrifice themselves. So dramatic. She raised an eyebrow at me, fully serious. I wanted to be able to turn to my right and share a knowing look with Hailee, but she was icing me out like I was the one who'd hurt her. The thought of it made me even angrier.

"Deal. Let's do this," I said, fixing Olivia with a determined look of my own.

Olivia ran out from behind our cover screaming like she really was an action star. As promised, she hit Charlie in the leg, taking her out, but Charlie hit her in the arm at the exact same time, both of them falling like they'd been hit with real bullets. I laughed as quietly as I could before getting into position.

After a few deep breaths, I ran out, catching sight of Hailee who had just tried to make a run for it from a rock she must've been hiding behind. After hitting her in the stomach with my paintball gun, she fell back a little from the force of it, her ponytail swishing as she went. Hailee was sitting up by the time I walked over to her, extending my hand. She swatted my hand out of her way and stood.

"Okay," I said, stepping back to give her space. She wiped her jeans and looked at her shoes. I could feel the others' eyes on us, waiting with bated breath, just like I was. She was close enough that I could smell the lavender from where I stood, but it didn't smell right, clouded by my anger. "So, you're really not going to say anything?" I asked, shifting my weight from left to right so I wouldn't ache too much later.

"What is there to say?" Hailee asked, the annoyance dripping like an ice cream cone from her voice. I scoffed at her. Maybe she had a selective memory, but I was there, and I remembered being kissed and then forced to watch as my world was pulled out from under me by the person I'd always thought was the biggest part of it. And yet, Hailee was still watching me like I was the one who'd hurt her. That was rich.

"*I'm sorry, Andrea*, is a great place to start," I spat out. Hailee placed both her hands on her hips, stepping toward me. She looked at our friends, who were probably looking away now and pretending that they weren't listening in, but I kept my eyes on her.

"I have nothing to be sorry for. You wanted space before—well, now, so do I," she said loudly, moving to walk past me and off the course. If that's how she wanted things to be, fine. Two could play this game. But I had more to say, so I followed her.

"You're a coward," I yelled. By now, the other paint-ballers waiting to suit up were looking at us curiously, not just our friends. We pressed on. Hailee whirled around to face me, anger and a hint of hurt clouding her features.

"And you're a liar," she yelled back.

"Me? A *liar*? You're lying to everybody here—including yourself. But don't worry, Hailee, I won't tell them what happened last night. I know what a mistake it was," I shot back, before taking off my gear and pushing past her.

"Shut up, shut up!" Hailee screamed as we all reached the parking lot, storming around me so we were face-to-face again.

"Don't you ever touch me again," I yelled, the tears at the edges of my eyes begging to be set free now.

Olivia cut in, stepping between us. "You guys, calm—"

"Stay out of this!" we shouted back in unison. Olivia backed away with her hands in the air. The others walked over to comfort her. I looked back at Hailee and wiped the tears that had slipped through my resolve.

"Don't worry, I won't," Hailee spat, before stamping off. We all watched as she got in her car and drove away without another word. We stood in silence for a moment more. Finally, Olivia let out a loud breath and tucked her hair behind her ear.

"That is not how I saw this going," she said with an awkward chuckle. Charlie, Merv Jr., and Fiona all nodded in agreement.

"What?" I asked incredulously. Everyone shifted their eyes away from me even as I stepped toward them. Charlie picked invisible lint off of her shirt while Fiona found something interesting on the ground. The only person who looked as confused as me was Merv Jr. What were they all agreeing with? Why was I the last to know?

"Well, I kind of lied and told Hailee you wouldn't be here so she would come. I thought if you two were face-to-face, you could just talk it out, but instead you had a screaming match in the parking lot. I'm surprised we haven't been banned," Olivia concluded. I rolled my eyes and turned from her to the others.

"Were you all in on this?"

Everyone but Merv Jr. nodded their heads.

"In on humiliating me?" I continued. Olivia scoffed.

"Now you're being dramatic. We tried to fix it for you, Andrea, and it didn't work. I don't know the full extent of what you did to Hails, but sue me for trying to help," she said. I turned back toward Olivia, who was glaring at me now.

"You can't be serious. This just made *everything* worse," I shouted, turning to everyone to make my point clear. I could feel a headache starting from my trying to hold back more tears, so I let them go.

"Well, you're not the one who sat on the phone with her while she cried for hours . . . we did," Olivia shot back. "Take responsibility for your part in this. You're not a victim, Andrea."

Charlie stepped forward.

"Olivia, that was uncalled for. You—"

I held up my hand and stopped her. No, there was no smoothing this over; it had been years in the making. A group of people came and went by us to the paintball spot, completely uninterested in the storm unraveling in front of them. I fixed Olivia with my best glare.

"Let her finish, Char. She's been waiting for this."

"Fine, we should all be honest here anyway." Olivia, decidedly disgusted, started right back up. "You pick people up and throw them away when you see fit, Andrea. I mean, look what you did to our friendship? One big fight and I no longer mean anything to you. You are always chasing after the next best thing, the next big adventure. Is that why you suddenly decided George mattered more to you than Hailee? Maybe the reason Hailee kissed you and instantly regretted it is because she knows you're fickle. You'll just drop her the second something else or someone new and shiny comes along. Just like you dropped me, huh?" Olivia asked.

"Olivia, what the fuck . . ." Fiona said.

"You're the saddest person I have ever met, Olivia," I hissed back, desperate to hurt her. "How do you even find the time to think about me and what I do? Maybe with all the free time you've had? You know, ever since I stopped you from mooching love and care off of my family, since yours doesn't even care about you?" I watched as she took a step back in shock.

"Choke," she shot at me.

"Show me how," I shouted, toward her retreating back. Fiona and Charlie shook their heads, in obvious disappointment, as I fought to regulate my breathing. Everything felt like it was falling apart, and I had been left with the debris. But despite my hurt, and righteous indignation, I was now asking myself if Olivia was right about me—and if Hailee was too.

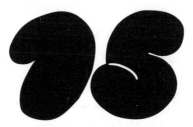

"Here you go, have a nice day," I said to the redhead who'd ordered mint chocolate chip ice cream.

"Thanks, uh, you too," she responded, and dropped a five-dollar bill in the tip jar. I went for a smile in thanks, but when the next customer winced at my awkwardness, I knew I hadn't been successful. I had only been at work for two hours, and I was already ready to go home. I took four more orders until Michelle, the shop's namesake—a light-skinned, tall and thin Black woman—came over and tapped me on the shoulder, telling me to come to the back office when things started to die down.

It had been a week since the paintball disaster. I hadn't spoken to anyone after Merv Jr. dropped me off at home. I'd needed to clear my head, but nothing helped. Since then, I hadn't been sleeping well, and I felt my body aching in agreement with my heartache. On top of everything, Hailee and I had always shared our shifts, but she hadn't been here this week and wasn't here today. So much of me wanted to forget that Hailee even existed—that the heartache was just a dream.

I took a deep breath and made my decision. I was going to continue my summer regardless. There was joy maybe somewhere in these new moments, in my new reality apart from Hailee. In order to find it, I couldn't keep saying her name, or thinking about her every second, or waiting for things to be okay again. Maybe it wouldn't be the best summer ever, but it could be a summer that I enjoyed.

"I can manage out here if you want to go see Michelle," Kacey, my coworker, said. This was our first time working at the shop together, but she seemed nice. She was a white, brown-haired twentysomething with wide-rimmed glasses she had to keep pushing up and off of her nose, and the kind of person you'd expect to see working at a library, not an ice cream shop. Today, though, I'd learned that she and her boyfriend were working two jobs each this summer to afford an apartment off campus when they went back to school in the fall. So, as far as first impressions went, she was very sweet, but she was quiet too, so I didn't try to push her into too much conversation. Luckily for her, we had gotten busy immediately.

I thanked my coworker and headed to the back to talk to Michelle. When I got to her office, Michelle turned to face me in her chair, motioning to the one across from her for me. I took a steadying breath as she crossed her legs and looked at me with a mixture of curiosity and kindness.

"Hey, kiddo. I can tell you're not having the best day . . ." Michelle trailed off as I looked past her to a picture of her and Peter, her husband, with their two tiny dogs. When he hired Hailee and me, he told us the story of how they met at their high school's first decathlon team meeting. Michelle turned to follow my line of sight, and no one could've missed the way she lit up. She turned back to me, quickly schooling her features.

"No, I'm not. I'm sorry, Michelle," I said. I had slept terribly the night before and I was sure the bags under my eyes could be seen from space. After the tears dried up this morning, my resolve had come roaring in; in my mind, Hailee and I were going to talk today: a week was enough time to cool off, remind ourselves that the thing that mattered most was our friendship, and finally smooth things over. My heart had been broken into a million little pieces a week ago, but we were supposed to fix it. But Hailee wasn't here to fix this. Hailee wasn't here. "I'm not usually like this, it's just that last week—"

Michelle raised her hand to stop me and smiled gently. Normally, I'd worry that a gentle smile was being used to infantilize me, but not with Michelle—she never treated me like I couldn't do something just because I was disabled. I appreciated that.

"Don't mention it. When Hailee called out again early this morning, I thought you were going to call out too. I was young once—I remember pretending to be sick so I could spend the day with my friends." She laughed, lost in a memory for a moment. I let her hang there while I digested what she'd said. Hailee called in sick? Of course she did. She'd been fine last week when she kissed me and ran like I was the biggest mistake she'd ever made . . . but whatever.

"Anyway, maybe she is actually coming down with something if you two aren't together. And I mean this with only love, but you look exhausted, Andrea. Your next shift isn't until next week anyway, so I called Peter—we'll cover this shift so you can go home and rest." She finished and patted my arm softly before she left the room with a final wave.

I texted my mom to ask her to pick me up. I sat outside on the bench in front of the shop. The sun was trying its best to keep me company, but I needed to be alone for a little while before my mom got here. She pulled up when I was a few levels into my match-three game. She smiled at me softly.

"Breakfast?" she asked when I was in the car with my seat belt buckled. I nodded wordlessly and she pulled out. Breakfast was my favorite meal to eat at any time of the day. Maybe it would help me feel better. Two streets from the restaurant, she grabbed my hand and started rubbing soothing circles with her thumb; I realized I was crying. Mom turned on the radio for the rest of our ride to Deb's, our favorite diner with all day breakfast, and the best scrambled eggs in the tristate area. My dad would have disagreed, of course, but he always cleared his plate when we went.

This was the first time Mom and I had ever gone alone though, in my memory at least, and it felt good to be spending some time just with her, circumstances notwithstanding. Even though my parents had moved to our small town for privacy before they had me, it still felt like I was always having to share Mom with the die-hard fashion fans and internet eagers desperate for pieces of her that they didn't deserve. In some way, I understood the excitement—Mom was everything good they thought she was, and more. She's an icon. Still, I felt very protective of her and her desire for privacy. We were four steps inside Deb's when a lanky, well-dressed Black man approached us.

"I'm sorry to do this, but my name is Sean, and I just wanted to tell you that I love your clothes so much. I'm even wearing your jeans and shirt and jacket right now," he said. "But you knew that, sorry . . . um . . ." Mom gave him her most comforting smile, and they took a big, deep breath together.

"Hi Sean, it's nice to meet you. I'm Evelyn. I'm here with my daughter so I can't stay and chat, but would you like a picture?" She said this as though she were just as excited at the prospect as he would be. I politely excused myself and found our usual table empty. After the picture was done, Mom came over and sat down quickly.

"He seemed nice," I said. "And honestly, they all do, but . . . aren't you exhausted by that?"

I asked, because I was. I picked up the salt and pepper shakers and played with them for a moment. I heard my mom blow out a breath, so I gave her a second to think it through, then put the shakers down and looked at her.

"It's been a long time since anyone asked me that," she answered with a sad smile. The waitress came and took our orders, then I put my arm across the table to grab her hand and squeezed it. I silently waited for my mom to smile again, a real one this time.

"I can start saying no for you if you'd like?" I asked, shrugging as she giggled. Honestly, it would be easy. I looked around the restaurant and was pleased to find that no one else cared that Evelyn Williams was here, though, and we certainly weren't going to draw any attention to ourselves and change that. This was our time.

"My own personal bodyguard, huh?" Mom asked, the light back in her eyes. She smiled as the waitress brought our food and left quietly. I dug into my omelet and cut it in half very sloppily. The whole limited-range-of-motion thing that came with my disability caught up to me sometimes. Mom took the other half and gave me half of her pancake stack. We said cheers with the pieces of bacon and talked about how delicious the meal was. As tired as I felt, everything was great right here in this moment, until I took the last bite of omelet and my mom cleared her throat.

"I want to talk about Olivia," she said, her voice changing as she set her silverware down. She was willing to ruin a perfectly good afternoon, talking about the very person who took stock in ruining her daughter's life.

"We could do literally anything else. Let's talk about bugs, math, the stock market, ummm . . . drowning," I begged. I'd happily relive every embarrassing moment in my life so far. Mom always loved to plan ahead, maybe we could plan for the next school year. "What do you want for your birthday? Let's discuss."

"Andrea Monet W—" Mom started.

"Fine, what about her?" I asked, cutting in. The faster I could ask, the faster this would be over with.

"Remember . . . remember that story I told you about the time your grandparents went on that family vacation without me?" Mom asked, and I grew angry at the memory. My grandparents were never kind to Mom in the short time I'd spent with them, before Mom cut them out of our lives for good. Even years later, as we sat here in this booth, Mom was clearly still so sad about it.

"Yes, you were seventeen, and they'd left on a whim after a call from a friend," I answered. From what I remembered, my mom had cooked, cleaned, and gone to school like it was a normal week. She'd told no one that her parents were gone and let everyone think nothing was wrong. A month later, Mom was scouted to model, and her life finally began.

"Well, it was like that all the time. So many people thought we had the perfect life, and that was because your grandparents liked to keep up appearances. But I always had a feeling that they didn't really want me—until my career took off. It broke my heart," she said wistfully. I watched Mom eat the last of her pancakes, and waited. There was no need to try and fill the silence. I knew there was more. I took the last sips of my raspberry iced tea and picked at the rest of my half of the pancake stack, though I was full and more interested in what Mom was trying to get at. When she was done eating, I encouraged her to continue.

"You see, the thing with Olivia is . . . that is her life too. Everyone, including you"—she paused and looked at me pointedly; I shrunk a little under her gaze—"looks at her like she has it all, because she has money, popularity, talent, and whatever else . . . but none of that replaces love. She's lonely, and desperate for acceptance and love from two people who only want to give it when it suits them best," Mom finished. She picked up a napkin and dabbed her eyes. I reached out to grab her hand, but she shook her head.

"Oh," I said, letting the new information settle. I knew that I was lucky to have parents who loved me unconditionally, but I realized I never really stopped to think about what it was like to not have that. I'd tried so hard not to think of Olivia when she and I ended our friendship, because I told myself that our friendship probably never meant anything real to her in the first place. All the things she'd said last week to hurt me, though—that had been unfair. "But at paintball she—"

"I know, she told me exactly what she said. When you two stopped being friends—real friends, not whatever you two are passing off now—she lost the only family that loved her," Mom said. I chewed on my lip and took my time looking everywhere but her. There was a couple across from us who looked to be on a first date, and a family in the booth in front of them laughing about a water-rafting trip. I would never want to do that. The most I ever did when we went to Charlie and Fiona's lake house was ride on the back of one of their Jet Skis. Well, that, and play chicken.

Our group had had so many good times at that lake house. I thought about the good times we were all supposed to have this summer, and though it wasn't even nearing its end, it felt like all the plans I'd had were crumbling at my feet. I could feel Mom eyeing me with concern, and I realized she expected me to respond. I took a few moments to remember what she had just said.

"I can't believe she's telling you things," I replied. "About your own daughter." Could nothing stay between the group anymore?

"She has no one else," Mom said simply.

"I guess I never thought Olivia truly went without," I shrugged. Mom sighed and patted my hand before paying the bill, and we left the restaurant. I grabbed her arm—not for support, like I led her to believe—but because I wanted to. We walked to the car and got in.

"Everyone thought the same about me, but I went without the thing I wanted most," Mom said. She squeezed my hand and put on her own seat belt. Had I been looking at this the wrong way? I'd spent so many years believing that the reason my friendship with Olivia ended was that Olivia thought she was too good for me. Don't get me wrong, I scoffed at the idea—and was absolutely still angry—but behind that anger was something else.

"Behind your anger is hurt," Mom replied when we hit a red light. I looked at her profile in shock.

"What? I asked, keeping my eyes on her.

"You were thinking out loud again," she answered. "Don't look at me like that. I know that's what it is because that's what it was for me. As angry as I was with my parents, I was hurt more."

"I have got to stop doing that," I said, out loud but more to myself than anyone else. Mom's laugh pulled a smile out of me as she turned the corner. We were two streets away from home. I nodded my head, the decision made.

"Honey, please don't stop being exactly who you are," Mom replied, cringing at her own cheesiness, but I just beamed at her anyway.

"Hey, could we actually stop somewhere first?"

I got out of the car, turned around to the window, and told Mom I'd see her in a bit. She gave me a thumbs-up and I watched her drive off. When she was out of sight, I took a deep breath and walked up to the steps. I knocked on the door and waited. Seconds later, it swung open, to Cathy Livingston.

Olivia's mom was a skinny white woman with dyed-blond hair and an air of self-importance to match it. She smiled at me softly. When we were kids and Olivia still had sleepovers, her mom had let us play with her makeup and wear her clothes, even when she was there, which wasn't often. But we'd had Annie, Olivia's nanny, to spend time with, so I'd sort of always thought everything was great for Olivia. As I looked at Cathy and her designer clothes, her "youthful" face with dead eyes, I realized maybe I'd been wrong about that too. Olivia's dad, Philip, was at least ten years Cathy's senior. The few times that I'd seen them when I was old enough to recognize what love was, they'd never seemed like they were in it. Philip liked to keep his distance from my family and his own. Still, I'd always thought Olivia's mom seemed like the coolest person, always on the go, never staying in one place too long. Now though, that just seemed exhausting.

Mom had traveled a lot too when we were young kids, but she'd always been there when it counted. And the older I got, the less she traveled. Or she took us with her so she wouldn't miss much. I'd always wanted a trip or adventure to look forward to, and I was just a kid, so I thought Olivia had that with her parents—without realizing at the time that they almost always left her behind. I didn't see how unfair it was that she was always having to say goodbye to them and having to make excuses for them not attending any school function or activity. But now I did.

"Hey sweetie! Haven't seen you around in quite a bit," Cathy said. She tapped her foot absent-mindedly, but quickly.

"It's nice to see you too! I was actually wondering if Olivia was home? And how are you and Philip?" I asked. They had never wanted any one of us to address them formally. Both Cathy and Philip said calling them Mr. and Mrs. Livingston made them feel old.

Cathy stepped aside and welcomed me in; I walked past her, though I was genuinely curious about how they were doing. Even after Olivia and I had agreed to tolerate each other for the benefit of our friends, I was the only one who knew what the inside of her house looked like—I was the only one who Olivia had let spend any real time with them. The other girls wondered, even Hailee, but I always figured it wasn't my information to share.

"Listen, we're great, everything is great. I have to get back to my room, but Livy is up in hers. It was good to see you," Cathy said, patting me on the arm before walking down the hallway and letting her bedroom door close with a bang. I took another deep breath, taking the house in for a second. The trip to Olivia's room didn't take long. I was surprised to find that I still knew the way like the back of my hand. Despite evidence of a remodel, the things that mattered had stayed the same. The sunroom was to my right, and the first sitting room to my left. Down the hallway was the second sitting room, and just past that was the kitchen. A few more steps put me in front of a staircase, and I took the steps, slowly practicing in my head what I was going to say. Before I knew it, there I was, standing in Olivia's open doorway as she sat at her bay window, reading. I knocked on the wall beside me to make my presence known. Olivia looked up, sighed, and put her book down.

"What could you possibly want?" she asked coldly. I didn't blame her: our last meeting had been intense, at best. I took the shot, but kept on going—I deserved it. I walked into her room and stood by the ottoman at the end of her bed, waiting. I wasn't going to sit unless I was invited, and as much as I hated to admit it, this could go either way—she might have every right to throw me out. Olivia finally gestured in front of her face exasperatedly. I smiled at her gently and took that as my cue to sit. We watched each other, Olivia's question still unanswered.

When we were kids, we had spent hours sitting at that bay window, dreaming about who we would get to be, who we could love, and who would regret ever being mean to us. Now that I stood here in front of it again, for the first time in years, I realized her parents were who she meant when she said she had to always prove herself to people. At the time, I'd agreed, even though I wasn't sure who she was referring too.

Olivia had obviously expanded the bay window in the years since, so she could lie and read by it. Olivia loved books— she brought one with her everywhere. I wondered what she read now when she was upset, happy, angry, or needed an escape? There was so much I didn't know anymore about the girl before me. Worse, I realized I wanted to know again so badly. The thought left a pang in my chest.

"I know we haven't always seen eye to eye, Olivia. But I need your help," I pleaded, scooting further back onto the ottoman. Olivia crossed one leg over the other and sat straighter. The thin line of her mouth made me think this was already certain to be a losing battle, but I had to try.

"You came here asking me for help?" Olivia laughed loudly, clapping her hands together. "Who let you in anyway?" she asked. Annoyance lacing her voice as she uncrossed her legs and slouched a little.

"Your mom, on her way back to her room." I paused as Olivia smacked her lip. "She always liked me. You know that."

"That makes one of us," Olivia snarked. I deserved that shot too. This wasn't going to be easy, and that's why it mattered so much. I had a lot of making up to do for the hurt I'd caused Olivia over the years, and at the paintball day. I had been hurt by Olivia throughout the years too, and at paintball day, but I wasn't here to rehash who hurt who worse, because at the end of the day we both lost, and my hurt didn't take away how sorry I was for hurting her. "Why are you here, Andrea?"

"I was hoping we could talk," I blurted out quickly, nerves really getting the best of me. *I miss you . . .* I couldn't say that yet.

"About what?" Olivia asked. I could maybe see the ice thawing the longer she watched me, and saw that I wasn't on the defensive, or readying to attack her.

"Us. I'm sorry that I screamed at you and poured that green paint on your white birthday dress in middle school. I said a lot of mean things in that hallway, because I thought you were ashamed of me—"

"And I'm sorry for saying I was ashamed of being your friend back then. I've never been ashamed of you. I was just trying to hurt you," Olivia replied, crestfallen. The book she was reading lay open on her lap. She looked back at me when I started speaking again.

"You stopped coming around, and you wouldn't tell me why. We used to do everything together, and then you shut me out. I was hiding sadness behind my anger, and I'm sorry I started that rumor about you having a crush on Mr. Pearson. I'm sorry too I said you were mooching off my family because yours doesn't care about you."

"They don't care about me, clearly. You were right about me liking Mr. Pearson, though. He always waited with me when my parents didn't show, or were late. He had the prettiest green eyes too," Olivia said in a mockingly dreamy voice, before laughing open-mouthed with abandon. She took a quick breath to right herself. When she spoke again, her face was serious.

"It's wild how low the bar was to earn my immediate 'love.' You know, my parents actually hired Merv after Mr. Pearson threatened to call CPS? After they fired Annie for essentially threatening to do the same, after I'd called her crying. I'd woken up to them gone in the middle of the night, with a note that said they were headed to their third honeymoon. I heard them arguing about it one night afterwards. They were more concerned about what people might think, than the possibility that they could lose me." Olivia let a few tears fall before swiping them away angrily. Tears I wasn't sure I was supposed to see.

Olivia looked off to the side as if she was lost in a memory. That was the most she'd ever shared with me about her parents' neglect. Looking back, we had been so young.

"I didn't fully know what was happening," I said softly. "If I had known, maybe I—" I twiddled my thumbs for something to do. I didn't even know people still did that in stressful situations, but here I was. I'd abandoned her when she needed me most.

"You weren't supposed to know—that's why I stopped coming around."

"I get that, I do. But why did you come into art class that day and say, unprompted, that we needed to talk, only for you to tell me that you were tired of having to be my friend because I slow you down, and some other kids at soccer called you 'freak's friend?' Why did you let them call me that? Why did you say you were embarrassed to be seen with me?"

"I didn't let them say it, I defended you. But I didn't want you to know that. I didn't mean any of the terrible things I said that day, Andrea, But I said that I was embarrassed to be seen with you because I knew it would hurt you. I had to think quickly, because I knew if you found out how bad things were at home, someone would come and take me away, and I was scared to leave the only place I have ever known."

"Geez, Olivia, I—"

She stopped and raised an eyebrow. "And don't you go looking at me like that. Like you feel sorry for me. We're enemies," she said exasperatedly, but I heard the smile in her voice.

"Yes, sorry," I offered, crossing my legs and looking down at my shoes. A short silence stretched on, and we let it. I looked around her room, taking in the pictures that hung above her desk next to the window. There were some of her with her teammates, her aunt, and the five of us.

"I hated coming home to an empty house. I joined soccer. They still have only been to two games. I've been playing since middle school, Andrea."

"They don't deserve you," I said easily. She snorted at that, as if she didn't believe me. I had done a bang-up job of making her feel terrible for years. I moved my hands until they sat on my knees in front of me, uncrossing my legs. I watched as Olivia took in what I said and then started to respond. My hand went up to stop her.

"Let me finish please," I went on, waiting until she nodded in agreement before I continued. "My mom told me at breakfast why she thought I was being way too hard on you, and at first, I was angry. I thought she was supporting you over me or something. But I see it now. When you lost me, you lost her too." I took a sharp breath in at my own words, and so did she. I began to cry. There was still the small possibility she could laugh at me for showing her my emotions. But when I gave up watering the backs of my hands with my tears, I looked up to find Olivia was crying too. She moved quickly to come sit down next to me, looking me in the eye as she did.

"I thought you were replacing me with Hailee anyway, and I wanted to hate her, I tried—" Olivia said.

"But it's impossible," I cut in.

"Yeah," Olivia laughed. "She's really great but so are you. You said pretty mean things to each other, and now you both need to apologize and figure out whether your relationship is worth saving. I think it is." She took my hand and squeezed it. I kept her hand in mine and stared at her, tears fully falling down both our cheeks. She let go to wipe mine and replaced her hand with the other.

"I realize that now and I need to fix it, but I need to fix me and you first," I said, wiping my eyes for one final time. We separated from each other, and Olivia went back to her window while I stayed put.

"I know, Hailee and I talked about it on the phone last night. I called her to talk through what happened at the paintball place. Merv told me I took it too far, and she agreed. I told her she took it too far too, for the record. But that's a conversation you two need to have. I'm sorry for the terrible things I said about you cutting people off. I was just so angry at you for doing it to me." Olivia settled back at the window, smiling at me sheepishly.

"I'm trying to fix everything between all of us. I was thinking that we could fix it during the concert, maybe? Hailee won't come if I ask—if it's still on, even. Could you? Maybe she'll come and we can talk. I miss her," I said dejectedly. I lifted my foot and dug it into the hardwood floor and sighed.

"What's in it for me?" Olivia asked, standing and tucking a piece of hair behind her ear. She walked the short distance from the window to the ottoman and stood in front of me expectantly. Her arms were crossed in what looked like defensiveness, her signature soccer-game glare leveled at me though we were nowhere near the field.

"What could you possibly want?" I asked. We were too old for ponies, I did not have enough money for a new car, and she had a dishwasher already so I was *not* going to do her dishes. I cast my eyes down, thinking about what Mom had said, and what Olivia had lost when we stopped being friends—what I'd lost.

Olivia's glare turned into a bright smile. "Sorry, Drea. I guess it is too soon to tease you like that. I'll do it under two conditions—" she started.

"Anything you want."

"Great. One: I want to be invited to Sunday dinners again. And two: I want to be real friends again," she answered confidently.

"That's it?" I asked, smiling. At that moment, the sun floated its way through the window I used to love. "You got it."

I stood to leave, but Olivia lunged at me. I flinched a little, but instead, she wrapped her arms around me, tightly pulling her head down to rest on my shoulder. I squeezed her back with just as much excitement and relief. She released me eventually and walked back over to her bay window.

"You know your dad is the best cook in the county. If you want me to ask for more, I can," Olivia added, smiling for the first time too. She picked her book back up and opened to her page. She looked up at me, though, with the kind of smile she gave the girls: a genuine one. Being on the receiving end of one finally felt so nice.

"No, that's okay. Friendship it is. See you Sunday," I said, my smile so wide, I knew my cheeks would hurt later. Worth it. Happier than I'd been in weeks, I headed back out to my mom.

The next day I went through my normal morning routine, then texted Charlie and Fiona to see what they were up to. There was no need for us to continue not talking just because of everything that had gone down. After fixing my friendship with Olivia, I felt like I was one step away from everything going back to how it was before.

Andrea: Doing anything today?
Fi: Mall later. You coming?
Char: We need retail therapy
Andrea: Same. I need a dress, what time?
Char: 2?
Fi: 2:30

Char: Ugh. 2:30.

Andrea: See you two then. Haha

Our local mall was, surprisingly, pretty great. It was always full of people, and, despite the fact that we felt like the only teenagers who still liked going to the mall, we loved it. There were the power walkers in windbreakers, the parents shuffling their toddlers from store to store, the preteens walking around without supervision for the first time, and the three of us, arm in arm, despite having too many bags.

"Let's eat here. I'm starving and my legs are screaming at me to sit," Fiona announced after we had shopped a while. We walked back to the food court, which took us by Tulip's again. Tulip's was the kind of store made for Fiona. All tall ceilings, pop music, and femininity with an edge. Which was, coincidentally, the tag line for the store. Honestly, she might as well have applied for a part-time job she was here so much. They'd be lucky to have her.

"That's my line," I teased, unlinking our arms as Charlie laughed. I grabbed Charlie's bags as she turned to her sister.

"I'm going to run in and grab you that shirt, Fi," Charlie said. I smiled at them both. The only time I hated being an only child was when those two were being sweet to each other.

"You sure?" Fiona asked, excitement lacing her voice. She switched her bags from the left side of her body to the other. Fiona loved to mix hard and soft—like today, she'd paired her baby-blue sunflower dress with combat boots and a faux-leather jacket, despite it being eighty degrees outside.

"Yes, you two sit. I'll be right back," Charlie said. As we sat, we watched her combat boot-covered toes move through the store's entrance. Fiona and Charlie's footwear matched today. Though they never let you forget that they "are in fact our own people," they each often wore something that matched the other, even if it was just a shoe, bracelet, or jacket.

The last time we were at the mall it had been the five of us, arm in arm for Olivia's birthday in January. She'd wanted a new dress to take pictures in, and had her dad's platinum card and full permission to use it, because her parents had a last-minute trip they couldn't cancel for their daughter's birthday. The day was so perfect even Olivia and I weren't trading jabs—we were too excited to be with the people that we loved. Olivia was channeling the anger and annoyance she usually reserved for me toward her parents. She'd bought the dress she wanted and about one hundred other things. She wouldn't leave until we each agreed to let her buy us at least two things of our own, too. We ran around the mall for hours, and every time I needed to rest, Hailee did it with me, intertwining our fingers and cracking jokes.

"I'm really proud of you," Hailee said, squeezing my hand once before letting go. She'd smiled at me, and I literally gasped; I should've recognized then what those butterflies were. Hailee had laughed at me then, but it was in a kind way, like I'd said something funny. I'd watched the way her face lit up out of the corner of my eye. She placed her hand on my knee and the rest of the mall faded away.

"Why? I didn't do anything," I said, clearing my throat, forcing the mall to come back into view. I looked out in front of us, watching our friends' cash out at the register.

"For letting her have this day. I know she's not talking about it much, but I know it has to hurt."

"Yeah, her parents are seemingly always busy, but even I didn't think they'd skip her birthday. We can go back to hating each other tomorrow," I'd said with a grin, as Hailee smacked my arm.

"You don't really hate her. You couldn't even if you pretend to!" Hailee exclaimed. "I know you, and your heart is too big, Drea. And one day you'll let more than just us see it. One day you'll let Olivia see it again, and I'll get to say, 'I told you so,'" she teased, leaning into me from where she sat on my right side.

"You're so sure you believe in me that much?" I asked, skeptically, pressing my hands together between my thighs for something to do.

"Of course, completely," Hailee replied, certain. She nodded her head as though the decision was now final. Our friends were out of the store now and walking toward us. I stood first, linking arms with Charlie. As we headed toward the food court, I caught Hailee's eye again as she went arm in arm with the birthday girl, and when she winked at me, my insides turned to mush. I didn't recognize that was the feeling I'd felt then, but I recognized it now.

I fled from that memory and turned back to the conversation Fiona was having with me now about the food she was planning to get. She tapped my right foot the way Hailee normally did, or, the way she used to.

"Where'd you go?" Fiona asked. The concern creased her forehead.

"I was just thinking about the last time we were here," I said, smiling and meaning it.

"That was a really fun day, wasn't it? We were all so worried about Liv, but she ended up having a nice birthday." I followed her gaze and we watched her sister check out. "Don't tell her I told you this, but I love her a lot," she whispered conspiratorially. We both giggled at her "confession" as Charlie walked toward us, her eyebrow raised.

"Your secret is safe with me," I promised.

After eating an obscene amount at the food court, we walked back toward the car, dodging a few people that weren't really looking before they backed out of their parking spaces. As we sang along to some of the songs on the radio, our windows down and the sun shining on us, I felt like I was one with the passing trees. But nearing home, we started going by too many things that reminded me of the person I was trying to forget. I sang louder, stuffing down the remaining feelings as we hit my street, and then realized the fun didn't have to stop there.

"Hey, do you two want to go see that new rom-com tonight?" Charlie and Fiona exchanged looks, and I felt confused. Fiona turned down the music as they pulled into my driveway.

"Uhhh . . . we sort of already have tickets and plans to see it with Hailee tomorrow. Sorry," Fiona said. The guilt on their faces was actually kind of funny. There was nothing to be sorry for, though: I didn't want them to feel like they had to choose.

"Oh, no need to apologize; it's fine. I get it. I hope you guys have fun." I smiled at them both, hoping they knew that I meant it.

"We told Hailee she couldn't come today, if it makes you feel any better," Charlie blurted out. She covered her mouth with her hands but the words were already out. They looked at me like I was a ticking time bomb, but I said nothing. A small silence stretched on between us as a Megan Thee Stallion song started playing. I closed my eyes and joined in on a few of the lyrics. And I realized that, actually, it did make me feel a little bit better.

"Char," Fiona chastised, looking at me in the back seat. I wasn't sure why I hadn't gotten out of the car yet, besides a quiet desperation for them to understand that I was fine.

"Seriously, it's okay. It's one movie. We can do something some other time," I said with a shrug, finally getting out. I walked to the trunk to grab my bags and back to the passenger-side window to wave goodbye.

"Good luck on your date. It's Tuesday, George said, right? Let us know how it goes, yeah?" Charlie asked, throwing a cheesy thumbs-up with the question.

"Yeah," I said. "Text me when you get home?"

"Duh, love you!" Fiona turned the music back up and pulled out of the driveway, peeling down the street. I walked inside and brought my bags up to my room. After I put everything away, I headed back downstairs. My parents were sitting on the couch. They must've just come in from the back patio. I joined them.

"Hi, sweetie. How was the mall?" Mom asked, and I knew she was genuinely curious.

"Good, I got a lot of cute things," I said proudly.

"Try on later?"

"Absolutely!"

"Well, now that we got that out of the way," Dad started. "I was thinking that Tuesday night after work we could go to that mini golf place. It's been a while since I wiped the floor with—"

"I can't—I have plans," I cut in. "Besides, you don't beat, you cheat. Mom and I have already decided."

"What plans?" Dad asked.

"I'm going to dinner with a friend," I said, tucking my hair behind my ear. I knew he'd be a typical dad, even though this was the twenty-first century. I also knew I wouldn't have much trouble getting the yes to go. "His name is George Fallon, he's only one grade ahead of me, and it's just dinner."

"Is this the George that Hailee was upset about?" Mom asked. "Because . . ." I watched as she tried to work through something that I couldn't quite decipher, her black eyebrows furrowing for just a moment before she waved a dismissive hand at herself and waited for my answer.

"Yes, but it's just dinner," I reassured them, though I wasn't sure who I was reassuring—them or me. "Dinner at Talia's. I forgot to tell you and Dad. He's picking me up at 5:30 p.m., and he'll have me home by 7:30 or 8:00 p.m."

"Absolutely not. We don't know him," Dad said, crossing his arms like this was final. I looked to Mom and silently pleaded. She bit her lip like the decision was hard for her, but eventually she relented with an eyebrow raise to let me know that it was okay, but we would be talking about this later.

"Actually, honey, we do. Remember that kid who helped with the bake sale when the school was raising money for the art program?" I sighed in relief.

"The one who loved my eclairs?" I fought the urge to roll my eyes. Here I was asking to go on my first date and Dad was busy inflating his ego. I could actually see his chest rise in his green polo shirt. Men.

"Yes, that's the one. We'll re-meet him first of course, tomorrow before they go," Mom said, watching me sigh once more. I tried not to be too bratty—she was sticking her neck out for me while Dad was behaving like a caveman—but I was still a teenager, so they had to expect some attitude. "Briefly,"

Mom added for my benefit. She took my hand and squeezed it. I really did have the perfect mother. Don't tell her I said that though—she'll put it on a T-shirt.

"Fine. I'm not going to act like I like this, but I'm not going to be all macho about it either," Dad finished. He walked into the kitchen and opened the fridge. "I need to bake about it."

"Brownies?" I suggested, following him. He huffed, but pulled out the ingredients right after. "Love you!" I walked back to Mom and smiled. I let her grab my hand and lead me up the stairs to my room.

I hesitated at my door frame for a second. I couldn't take my eyes off the space between my bed and the dresser where I'd experienced the best and worst moments of my life in quick succession. I'd thought it wouldn't keep hurting to be in here, but the edge had not dulled. I closed my eyes and bit my lip, then walked quickly inside and stood near the dresser to avoid raising suspicion.

"I think you should wear those dark-blue jeans we never released from the fall line last year, and that cute flower top Hailee got you," Mom said, her back to me as she rummaged through my closet. I flinched at Hailee's name. "I'll do your eyebrows and you can wear a clear lip gloss. Do you want help with your hair?"

"Yes, thank you for asking," I said. Mom shrugged and turned around, satisfied. She laid the clothes on the bed so she could get a complete picture. The outfit needed shoes. When Mom stepped away from the closet, I spotted my black shoes with the heel small enough to keep me steady and comfortable. I grabbed them and Mom actually applauded me.

"Just what I was thinking—perfect." She put the clothes back in the closet but separated them so that they'd be easy to grab tomorrow, and closed the door. I had to admit—at least to myself—that my mom's excitement was contagious. I was really going to let myself have this.

"What does Hailee think about this date?"

"I don't know. We aren't talking, and I didn't ask her." I shrugged my shoulder to appear nonchalant, and opened my curtains. I felt tears rising, so I stood with my back to my mother and willed them away. I was not going to ruin this dress. Today I was wearing a bright yellow one with crisp white sneakers. The yellow looked great against my black skin, with a mother-approved "age appropriate" V-neck on the dress, and I didn't need my tears messing up the look. When I knew I had control again, I turned around.

"I think even though you two are going through . . . whatever you're going through, that she'd be happy for you," Mom reassured me, but I flinched again at the idea that Hailee would be happy about this date. Worse—the idea that she wouldn't care at all.

"I don't want her to know, Momma," I said, finally. The silence that followed sat carefully between us. I watched her nod and shrug. I wouldn't push it, of course, but I would be lying if I said I wasn't annoyed by the way she was poking and prodding.

"Fine. She is your best friend, but you don't have to tell her," Mom said. I moved to my bed and sat; Mom joined me.

"I'll tell her later," I lied, unable to keep my voice from rising an octave, appreciative of the fact that she said nothing else even though I knew she wanted to. In any other circumstance, the loyalty my parents had to Hailee would have made my heart soar, but right now it just made my eyes sting.

"Well, tell me about him. When did you two begin talking?" Mom asked, crossing her legs and smiling at me with excitement in her eyes that I knew well. Her giddiness pulled me out of my thoughts.

"We ran into each other at the art show in ShoeHorn. I was behind him in the line for food. He was funny and charming," I started, smiling at the memory. The honest truth was, there was a lot to like about George. Our easy banter, his gorgeous smile . . . and the kind of eyes you could get lost in. Sure, we didn't know each other well, but that's what dates were for. To get to know the person sitting across from you. I could do that—*we* could do that—and, who knew? Maybe he and I could be something special too. No pressure.

"You know your dad was much the same," Mom said dreamily.

"Go on, tell me the story again," I led her, putting my chin in my hand as we giggled. I gave my mother my full attention after promising she'd hear more about George after.

"It all began at my debut fashion show. I had just stopped modeling, and I was so nervous I almost threw up as it started. Unbeknownst to me, in the front row of all places, sat a man who didn't even want to be there. He was mumbling and groaning to the friend who'd invited him." Mom paused for dramatic effect, and we scoffed in unison like we always did at this part of the story. "Anyway, he shut up when he saw the clothes come down the runway."

"He sure did!" I encouraged. I could see it like a movie. Dad in the front row after working all day, dressed too casually in jeans and a white tee, flour on his cheek but so confident no one even cared. I could almost hear his grumbles.

"When the show was over and it was my turn to walk out with my clothes for the first time, you can bet I strutted for my life. On the way back down, as everyone was clapping and I couldn't keep the grin off of my face, I saw him and I knew he was it for me," Mom swooned. She unclasped her hands and let the stars leave her eyes.

"Love at first sight," I smiled, and rewarded her with the story of my first afternoon with George, skipping over the fight with Hailee that day because I had already cried to her about it. Mom didn't know it, but this was exactly what I needed.

I was never more grateful that Dad had gotten stuck working late than I was at this moment. Poor George sat on our couch politely nodding and smiling as Mom launched into the story about her first Paris runway show. I mouthed my apologies from where Mom could not see. George took it all in stride, winking like he'd planned for this. Still, I reminded my mother that George had made reservations that we were on the verge of missing, before she reminded me that Talia's was not that fancy and only did reservations for large parties. Checkmate. I was grateful she let us go after giving George "the third degree I promised your father." I told George I'd meet him at the car and hung back watching him go, then hugged Mom.

"Don't do anything you're not ready for," she whispered as she hugged me back. I squeezed her tighter.

"I won't, I promise," I said. I walked to George's car and got in. We drove off and my heart began to race. This was my first date, and I didn't want to mess it up, but every piece of advice I'd gleaned from teen movies was suddenly lost on me now.

George didn't seem to notice, thank God. We sang a few songs and the conversation flowed easily. In the car we covered favorite colors, music, candy bars, and sports teams. I shared that I inherited my love of the Yankees from my dad and George loved the Lakers because of his mother. I liked the way he laughed at his own jokes and didn't look at me while he drove, and I took the opportunity to study his profile. He caught me staring a few times at red lights and my heart would race a little again, but I didn't mind. I silently gave myself permission to put Hailee out of my mind as we arrived at Talia's.

When we were seated, I took a picture of the menu to post later because I had seriously neglected my socials and needed to share some content. The hostess took our drink orders and placed them down in front of us with a smile, before dashing away.

"I love this place," George said, taking a sip of his iced tea. I took a few seconds to people-watch and smiled at the old couple who walked past our table. I smirked when the woman gave me a thumbs-up. I looked back to George who I found smiling at me, his eyes twinkling. "I asked my parents every year for my birthday to come here instead of having a party."

"What do you love the most? The burgers or the chili?" I queried, fixing him with a pointed look before smiling. I sang along to the song coming from their speakers—an acoustic version of something I couldn't remember the name of—and let the candle light from the table frame my face. Honestly, the thing about Talia's was that it was like three types of restaurants in one. The food was the type you'd get at a sports bar; the decor led you to believe it was a dimly lit Italian restaurant—perfect for a first date; and the prices were reasonable. It was confusing but nice.

"I think it was more that my parents didn't fight as much when we came here," George said. I stopped singing and swaying immediately. Crap. I was going to go down as the worst date in history, who, despite not being flexible, put both feet in her mouth before we'd even ordered our food.

"I'm sorry I said that. I feel like such a jerk." I bit my lip and looked down at our wooden table. I could not believe how quickly I had ruined the night with my attempt at teasing. Being swallowed whole by the ground didn't sound so bad right about now, but then . . . George laughed.

"You're so cute when you panic," he teased back. I looked up at him skeptically, letting my left hand stretch across the table. A peace offering. When George squeezed my hand, I smiled. "It's fine, really. I even get two Christmases now, and their guilt got me my car, so it's fine." George shrugged and smiled once more, taking another sip of his tea. I removed my hand from his and reached for my otherwise untouched lemonade. I'd only taken a few sips when the waiter came over to our table.

"Hi, my name is Amber and I'll be your waiter tonight. Are you ready to order?" she asked. I was distracted by her hair. I was dying to dye mine her exact shade of purple, but so far, my parents were not budging, even though I'd been asking steadily for a year straight. If there was one thing I knew for sure, I'd eventually wear them down—I always did. Or turn eighteen, whichever happened first. George motioned for me to go. I pretended to tap my chin in thought, not even looking at the menu.

"Hi Amber! I'll have the cheeseburger sliders with bacon and a side of the loaded tater tots," I said, handing Amber my menu. She smiled like she was proud of my choice. I waited for George to order.

"I'll have the turkey club," he said easily, handing his menu over. He winked at me like we were in on something together, and I guess we were. Though he was laying it on a little thick, I was surprised to find that I was actually enjoying myself.

"Fries okay with that?" Amber asked.

"Perfect," George said. Amber walked away with our menus, and I promised myself that I would compliment her hair at the end of the night and not say anything else to possibly offend the cute boy sitting across from me. "Sliders, huh?"

"Yeah, they're really good here. Was I supposed to make a different choice?" I asked, taking more sips of my lemonade, but keeping my eyes on him, enjoying the way he squirmed a little.

"No, it's just most girls I know would've ordered a salad or something not as greasy," he replied, then realized that he was not going to get out of this easily. "What I mean is—"

I cut him off. "I like cheeseburgers, and before you say I'm not like other girls, let me reassure you that I am because we aren't special or superficial just because we order a salad or a cheeseburger. You know that, right?" I questioned, but didn't wait for him to answer. Instead, I fixed him with my best "this isn't working for you" look and took another sip of my lemonade.

"It's my turn to apologize. Sorry. You are right. I was being an ass," George said, chuckling awkwardly and running a hand through his hair. I hated how eager I was to forgive him, but then the secret last item on the basically abandoned Best Summer Ever list flashed before my eyes, and I decided: I couldn't find love if I gave up right after a teenage boy said something ridiculous. That, and I was finding his stammering charming. I chose to throw him an olive branch.

"Are you excited to be a senior next year?" In that moment I realized the gravity of what was happening: here I was, sitting across from the most popular boy in the school. Even if I hadn't been fighting with Hailee in some way about George, and trying really hard not to think of her, if this had been six months ago, even she would've thought I was joking at first. I was pretty sure no one would believe me outside of my core group of friends anyway. I would not even believe it myself, if I weren't actually living it.

"I know I should say yes, but to be honest? I'm more excited for the rest of summer and moments like this," George answered, and I playfully rolled my eyes. He laughed and continued on. "There is a lot of pressure on me at school. It's nice to get away from it."

I nodded in agreement—being "friends" with Olivia meant that I got a glimpse into how the popular kids lived, just by association—but even still, I couldn't really relate.

"I can only imagine. The fact that you want to get away from it all with me is the real surprise here," I laughed, but I could tell that George saw right through it. He shook his head fondly at me again and this time I didn't tell myself to look away.

"I won't pretend I know you like your friends do, but I can say that I want to," George said just as Amber came back over with our food. I watched him eat a few fries before I grabbed my first slider. I looked past him at the bartender pouring a couple of drinks, then turned my attention back.

"I want to get to know you too." I stuck my tongue out as he pretended like he had just won something. We kept eating our food in a comfortable silence, smiling when we caught each other staring. We ordered a piece of apple pie with vanilla ice cream to split for dessert. When we were finished, Amber came out with the check, and I complimented her hair as promised.

We talked for a few moments about how long it had taken to dye it.

"This may sound really weird, but are you Evelyn Williams's daughter?" she asked shyly.

"Yes," I said happily. I could tell that there was more she wanted to say, so I tried to encourage her with a smile.

"She's just a legend and I love her clothes. Can you tell her I said hi?"

"Can you convince her to let me dye my hair like yours?" I asked. We laughed, and I promised to tell her hello. I also told Amber that I would love to paint her if she were interested. George vouched for me teasingly and paid the bill. He grabbed my hand when we got up from the table and I liked the thrill of it all: my racing heart, the butterflies in my stomach, and even my slightly clammy hands. At the exit, when we thought we saw one of the co-captains of the soccer team, George dropped my hand and gave me the keys to go to the car while he went to the bathroom. I found the sudden change a little weird, but I tried not to think too much of it. When he got back to the car, he climbed in quickly and let out a breath.

"I was thinking," he said, "since this is so new and we really don't want anyone to get in the way of us getting to know each other—you know how high school can be—that maybe . . ."

He paused, his face turning slightly red as I waited. He tapped a beat on the steering wheel to a song I didn't know. I cleared my throat hoping to encourage him to continue.

"It would be best if we kept this a secret," George finished as we put on our seat belts.

"Keep this a secret?" I repeated, ignoring the pang in my chest. I wasn't asking for the world to know, but still: it stung.

"Yeah, I hope you don't mind. I just like the idea of this being for us right now, no prying eyes. Ya know?" he said, watching me to gauge my reaction. I plastered on a smile that could've won me an Emmy. The truth was, the item on my list said to fall in love—and if it wasn't going to happen with Hailee, I could work with George's stipulations. I'd have to. Who knew when I'd get this chance again?

"Yeah, it's fine," I replied, hoping I came across as sincere. George squeezed my hand again before he pulled out of the lot and began driving me home. I watched the cars pass. I loved this time of night when everyone seemed to be out and about. I put the window down and let my right arm hang out on the side just like I'd seen in the movies. I put the hurt of being a secret out of my head and sang along to the songs about feeling forever young and nights worth remembering. The thing about secrets was that they could be fun to keep—the rest didn't matter. And the way George looked at me when we were stopped made me feel like for the first time in my life, I was truly living.

He pulled into my driveway and turned off the car.

"I had a really nice time tonight," George said, looking over at me as I undid my own seat belt. The porch light turned on and I knew it was my mother's doing: she was so nosy. I looked him directly in the eyes before I responded. The night was still young, and I was grateful that this was all working out.

"Me too. You want to do it again?" I asked, feeling bolder and bolder as I leaned toward him. I noted the quick changes in George's face as I moved. First, there was the shock, followed by the awe, and then, the excitement as he moved to meet me halfway. He really was cute. I found myself excited too for what this could be if I let it happen. When our lips met, I felt a spark. A spark like a set of fireworks on the Fourth. And sure, it wasn't the same "world moving in slow motion" that I'd felt with Hailee, but when we pulled away, George didn't run.

I deserved and needed someone who was not going to run, so I smiled like the kiss meant the world to me. Even though it hadn't truly, yet, maybe it could someday. I willed some butterflies to appear and they did.

"Time and place. I'm there," George whispered as he looked at me. I ducked my head and bit my lip before meeting his eyes again. I opened the door but turned at the last second.

"Text me when you get home?" I asked. I got out of the car, and the wind picked up as I shut the door and leaned into the window. Out of the corner of my eye I saw the curtain move. My mother was not subtle in the slightest. I returned my attention to the green eyes in the car.

"Aw, you want to make sure I get home safely? You like me, huh?" George teased, and I tapped my chin again.

"I just want to make sure you can buy me food again," I teased back.

As I walked away and toward my front door, I reminded myself to stop thinking and just feel. What I was sure of was that it was a great first date, and I couldn't wait for another. When I looked back up from the ground, Mom was outside too and coming toward me.

"It was really nice. He was funny, charming, and sweet," I started, hearing George pull away, and making sure my enthusiasm matched hers. I told her all about the date, saving the waitress with the cool purple hair for the end in hopes that Mom's resounding excitement about the rest would get me a yes for my own hair. Instead, Mom congratulated me on the effort and wagged her finger playfully. It was worth a try.

"Your father and I will discuss a few streaks, but definitely not your entire head," she said. I would take every win I could. Back inside, I said goodnight to them and headed up to my room. I showered and put on my coziest pajamas. I climbed into bed and reached for my phone to check social media. Instead, I saw a missed text from Hailee.

Hails: Can we talk?

I read the text four times before it sunk in. I'd wanted her to say this very thing for what felt like forever. I'd even asked Olivia to help me make sure it happened soon at the concert. But despite the knot in my stomach, I wasn't sure now what I actually wanted.

My throat suddenly felt dry. I typed out "Yes. I miss you," before quickly erasing it and putting my phone back down.

I needed space from Hailee. I didn't have it in me to pretend like nothing had happened. The thought made me angry and hot tears began, but I wiped them away in favor of the resolve bubbling in me now. I didn't want to unleash my hurt on her again—that would just make me feel worse. So, time apart for a while definitely was the best choice for everyone involved. I waited until I could temper my feelings down before responding:

Andrea: I'm not ready.

George sent me a text a second later that he got home safe. I sent him back a smiley face and decided, at that moment, to give him my all. I wasn't going to spend every date night crying over her. I put my phone back down and was out like a light.

"UGH! This isn't working," I groaned out loud to my empty room. I'd been trying and failing for hours to come up with the perfect way to rework my self-portrait for the showcase. This year we were supposed to create our portraits with the words "Show Us Who You Are" as the guidelines. The problem was, every sketch felt like something was missing. This was useless—the thing I needed wasn't coming to me.

I couldn't take another third place trophy; I wouldn't. I'd grown so much since last summer. I needed to prove it.

I put down my sketchbook and walked to my bathroom to wash my face. The routine of it always relaxed me. My mom was always being sent face washes she didn't have time to try, so I was her guinea pig of sorts. Afterward, I walked down the stairs and joined my mom on the living room couch. My phone buzzed.

Hails: Okay, I get it. I'll try again in a few days.

I read the message twice and sighed before putting my phone back down and turning it over. When I looked back up, I saw my mom was looking at me and realized she'd seen the messages. I was grateful when she squeezed my hand and kissed my forehead before she left. Another buzz made me pick up my phone.

G: You, Me, Mini Golf tmrw?

I smiled because I loved mini golf, and I was good at it. I'd never played on a date before, but I was never going to be one of those girls in movies who threw their games to impress a guy. Actually, I didn't think they did that much anymore, which was great because it was a tired trope anyway and it meant I didn't have to. I decided to tease George a bit, though. After all, I was a naturally competitive person—blame my mother.

Andrea: As long as you don't cry when you lose
G: I don't lose
Andrea: We'll see about that.
G: Can't wait
Andrea: :)

"Go get dressed, we're going to be late," Dad said, appearing out of thin air. I looked at the date and time on my phone. I'd forgotten we had our monthly cooking class today. I rushed past him, ignoring his satisfied smirk.

~~~

At the entrance to my dad's restaurant—the one he'd built from the ground up before I was born—was a picture of my parents; my uncle Dennis, who has been my dad's best friend since middle school; and a few other workers on the night the restaurant opened. Above that picture read the words *D&D's Soul Food*. I always stopped and smiled at the picture.

My dad walked in without doing the same. I knew he was proud though. He talked about it all the time: how hard they'd worked, that terrible first year—the one offset by a bases-loaded, bottom-of-the-ninth, down-by-three-and-a-home-run-wins-the-game second year. By year four, I was born, and that was that. I walked over to the bar and sat in front of it. I saw the shadow of a very tall and muscular man out of the corner of my eye. When I yelped, that shadow had the audacity to laugh at me. I spun my stool to give him a dirty look as he came into view. In front of me stood a Black man with curly black hair, a full sleeve of tattoos, and a mole on his right cheek. To say he stood was a bit of a stretch, though, because right now he was hunched over with laughter.

"Hey Unc," I said, rolling my eyes as he composed himself. I was still fake pouting when he rounded the bar and picked me up, pulling me into a bear hug like he hadn't seen me in years, when it had been really just a few months. I laughed as he spun me.

"Hey Little D," Uncle Dennis said, placing me back on the ground and rubbing the top of my head. I made a face and fixed my hair, but I wasn't really upset. I'd missed him too. I sat on the stool in front of the bar as he went back behind it and poured me a Sprite. "How's my favorite niece doing today?"

"I'm your only niece, Unc," I said. Sure, I wasn't doing great, but he didn't need to know that. Dad walked back out to grab more chairs for the back room where the lesson would be. We watched him for a moment.

One of the things that always made me swell with pride about my parents was that they were always trying to make sure that I was exposed to people who looked like me, and who also understood things about me that they couldn't—hence the cooking class for disabled kids. They could be a little heavy-handed at times, especially when they should've known that I was only going to spend my time with Faye and Vanessa, but as an only child, I appreciated the effort.

"I told him to let one of the busboys set up the room, but he insisted on doing it himself," Uncle Dennis said, shaking his head and refilling my glass.

"He'll be sorry when he gets home later and Mom has to ice his back," I snickered, as Dad came back out for another set of chairs. Dennis let out a howl of a laugh, clutching his stomach. I laughed too, grateful that my mood was lifted and the lifters of it had no idea what they'd done. I loved being at the restaurant, and I was going to focus on how fun tonight would be—nothing else. I hadn't seen Faye and Vanessa in over a month.

For Christmas vacation last year, Vanessa and her moms had rented out one of the few accessible cabins in the area and we'd all stayed there for a week, eating s'mores and having snowball fights. Vanessa opted out of getting the wheels on her chair dirty, but Faye hit her with one anyway. We often talked about school, and the fact that no matter how much we loved our non-disabled family and friends, the truth was being disabled was really only something we understood with each other. So, on bad pain days, I called Faye and Vanessa, and they called me. We supported each other when we felt out of place.

"I'm going to go help Old Man Willie," Uncle Dennis said, tapping my shoulder before picking up a folding table with ease. Uncle Dennis stayed in such great shape—he was always dragging Dad to the gym and on hikes. My dad wasn't out of shape himself, but he had a bad back so he really shouldn't have been lifting anything heavy. I watched the two of them laughing as Uncle D swatted him away from another folding table.

Uncle D and my dad had been born a month apart, and he never let my dad forget it. They grew up with each other in New York City and were the closest thing to a sibling each would ever have. They'd found a shared love for cooking when their parents worked late, and they had declared on graduation day that they would open their own restaurant together one day—and they did. After my dad met my mom and they decided to move here, Dad convinced Uncle D to come, too. Dad and Uncle D decided this would be a perfect place for a restaurant and the rest is history.

A little while later Dad and Uncle Dennis came out of the back and sat on either side of me. I looked at my phone and saw that the time read 2:15 p.m. I raised an eyebrow at Dad, who at least had the decency to look sheepish.

"So, that didn't take as long as I thought it would," he said. I could've absolutely gone to the mall with Mom or something before class. Dad really needed to learn how to let go of control.

<p style="text-align:center">~~~</p>

Faye, a tall, skinny, redheaded white girl with hazel eyes and freckles on her nose was the first to arrive. I ran to hug her, nearly knocking us both over, and would have if it weren't for Faye's rainbow-colored cane. We laughed and walked over to the bar with her mother, Jenny. I hugged her too, and complimented her earrings.

"Love the new hardware, Faye!" I looked the cane over with appreciation. Faye flipped her red hair and admired it too.

"Shipped over from Milan, first class," Faye said fancily. I shook my head as though this news were obvious, before we began laughing again. "It was the best-looking one my insurance was willing to cover," she added.

"She got tired of the neon," Jenny interjected. I knew that Faye treated her canes like the seasons of runway fashion, and that she changed them as she saw fit, to match her mood or the phase she was in. The neon popped up after she'd struggled to feel like she was really being understood at school.

"The rainbow works for who I am now," Faye said easily. I hated that I couldn't be there for her the way she deserved at school. The kids were so cruel to her, and Faye's principal had to be strong-armed into doing something about it. Faye was in a much better place now, though, with her feelings toward herself and her autoimmune disease. Right now, her dream was to be an actress, so her wardrobe was flashy and loud, and she was much more outgoing and willing to meet new people. She was even going to join her community theater, which was a far cry from where she was last year. Before Vanessa or I knew that something was really up, Faye had begun dressing in neutral colors and warm tones, like she was desperate to blend in, and spent the year preparing for her future as a private investigator. This meant that whenever we were together, last year, Faye was always asking too many questions, and convinced that something was "afoot" even when we were just baking cookies. We loved Faye, so of course we were supportive, but the relief we felt when it was over was glorious.

Dad hugged Faye and Jenny before they walked to the back. I hung out with Lisa, the maître d' at the podium, waiting for Vanessa who lived the farthest away and was always the last to arrive. Other people attending the class walked in, and I gave them polite smiles because we were in my dad's restaurant, but I stayed right where I was. I couldn't move anyway, because I was in the middle of a rousing round of twenty questions in an effort to confirm that Lisa was seeing Jason, one of the cooks at the restaurant. I had seen the two of them getting cozy with each other the last time I'd been here. I'd gone outside to grab my dad's phone and saw them kissing against Jason's car. I'd texted Hailee immediately and we'd made up their whole dating timeline in our heads. Now that Lisa was very quietly confirming it, I was both excited and let down, because I couldn't even text Hailee about how right we were. Maybe one day I wouldn't itch to text Hailee while I was supposed to be taking space to figure everything out. It didn't feel like that day was going to be today.

"I have arrived," Vanessa sang when she and her moms Clarise and Holly were in front of Lisa and me. Vanessa, a short Black girl with shoulder-length braids, had her arms spread out like the end pose of an elaborately choreographed Broadway routine, and was already ready for the hug I rushed to give her. I hugged her moms too, and told Lisa I'd see her around, with a whispered promise that I'd keep her secret. We moved to the back room and Dad called me up front to join him. I smiled excitedly at the six tables in front of us. Faye was with her mom at one table, Vanessa was with her moms at another, and the other four tables were people I didn't know.

"Welcome, everyone," Dad said in his most professional voice. "My daughter and I are very happy you could make it today. Aren't we, Andrea?"

"Yeah, thank you everyone for coming out," I said from where I stood beside him, making funny faces at Faye and Vanessa until he turned to me to tell me that he could see me out of the corner of his eye. Oops.

Everyone snickered and Dad waited a few more seconds before he spoke again. "We're making monkey bread today!" He bowed when everyone clapped, which made us all laugh again.

"In front of you on your tables are one-half cup of granulated sugar; one teaspoon of cinnamon; biscuit dough; one-half cup of walnuts for you, Vanessa, and a half cup of raisins for you, Faye; one cup of firmly packed brown sugar; and three-quarters of a cup of butter, melted," I said. Even though I wasn't taking part in the actual making of the monkey bread, I was still excited to be at the head of the room—in the know—like my dad. I'd never tell him that though; he'd never let me live it down. He smiled at me like he'd read my thoughts anyway and walked to each table.

~~~

"Great job, everyone! Let me go run these to the oven—I'll be back." My dad grabbed a few pans of the bread, some of the parents offering to help too, and left the room.

"*Top Chef* is shaking," Vanessa said, wheeling away from her table and toward Faye's table.

"I noticed how quiet they've been since we started cooking today," I encouraged. I took Faye's mom's seat while Vanessa made a joke about having her own. The other tables were talking amongst themselves. Dad would probably tell me he was "disappointed" that I was spending my free time with people I already knew, but I wasn't up to meeting new people today, so he would just have to be disappointed. Once the three of us were seated and out of parental earshot, we talked about how happy we were it was summer. Everything was going great; light and easy the way I needed it to. Until Faye changed the subject.

"How is that real cute best friend of yours, Drea? We haven't seen or heard anything about her in awhile," she asked, and I flinched. I couldn't even deny I'd done it either. I cursed internally and reminded myself to stop doing that. I looked away from my friends for a second and took a breath.

"She's fine," I said, finally.

"Uh-oh," Vanessa replied.

"What?" I asked, watching as Faye and Vanessa exchanged looks like I wasn't there.

"Something definitely happened. That pause was too long, and we usually can't get you to shut up about her."

"That's not true," I answered Vanessa weakly. I knew that they were right, but I was trying to just be in the moment today with the friends I basically never got to see. A look between them said I wasn't going to get off that easily.

"Remember how she spent Christmas smiling way too hard at her phone before video chatting Hailee and making everyone be on their best behavior?" Faye said conspiratorially.

"That's because you two play way too much," I laughed, and Vanessa flipped her short, brown hair while Faye shrugged her shoulders.

"You love us," Vanessa said. She leaned in to whisper: "Now hurry up and tell us what happened before they come over here to 'check in.'"

I looked over at my friends' parents and knew that Vanessa was right. It wouldn't be long. I took a deep breath and let it go. I waited a second to gather my words, then closed my eyes. The trouble wasn't that I was afraid of their responses. It was that I couldn't even think about it without crying . . . so how was I supposed to say it aloud?

"We kissed, and then we fought. But we kissed," I whispered, watching them as this news sunk in, their faces changing from shock to pride. Faye started clapping and Vanessa gasped.

"Oh my God," Vanessa exclaimed, clamping her hand over her mouth as the parents looked over at us. Vanessa looked back and smiled reassuringly. "I mean, oh my gosh, Faye, why'd you spoil the next episode of *Riverdale*!" she clarified loudly, tossing me a thumbs-up. When they turned away, I smacked Vanessa's arm.

"Sorry, Drea," she whispered. I shook my head to signal my forgiveness.

"She kissed me and then said it was a mistake, so I guess that's that. I haven't been ready to talk to her since," I murmured, smiling softly at Faye as she touched my arm.

"We're sorry, Drea. We were so sure it would happen for you two," Faye said. I scooted my chair over and placed my head on her shoulder. I wasn't sure if I should tell them about George, but I knew I didn't only want to tell half of the story. So I leaned in again.

"There's more," I went on, looking between them to see that they were on pins and needles. If the shoe had been on the other foot and either one of them had been telling me this story, I would've been too. "There's a boy named George who seems to like me and we have been seeing each other in secret."

"Forget *Riverdale*, this is *so* much better," Vanessa exclaimed. She cracked her neck and shook her head excitedly. "A love triangle."

"Not quite. Hailee doesn't want me that way, remember? I'm her mistake." I stuffed down the pang at saying it aloud as deep as I could. One look at my friends told me they could see it anyway.

"You're not a mistake. And are you sure that's what she meant by it?" Vanessa asked, her facial expression neutral, but the hand she reached out for me to hold on to, supportive. Faye nodded in agreement. They watched me for a moment before looking at each other. I wish I knew what they were saying silently.

"Should you be doing this, girl? Seeing this guy when you're clearly not over Hailee?" Faye put her hand on her cane like she was gearing to stand, but Vanessa and I knew that she just liked to know it was near her.

"I'm not sure for certain. But I think he could help me get over her, and then I wouldn't have to lose her. I can't lose her," I said softly. I looked back over at their parents, who were still talking and unaware of the conversation two table lengths over.

"Jeez, Drea, that's heavy . . . but I get it. Are you really sure Hailee meant to call you a mistake?" Vanessa asked, grabbing my hand softly.

"I'm sure," I answered, squeezing her hand for comfort.

"Okay. Just, please . . . just be careful with this George person," Vanessa said. I nodded and pulled us all in for a group hug. We wiped our eyes when we broke apart, and laughed at our own sappiness.

Dad and the other folks came bouncing in with the breads a little later and set them on a table that had been moved into the middle of the room. Faye, Vanessa, their parents, and I walked over.

"Behold your masterpieces!" Dad boomed like a chef on a cooking show. He *was* a chef, so one out of two wasn't bad. He clasped my shoulder before I went around the room and congratulated everyone.

"Let's dig in!" Clarise announced like she was teaching the class. She handed her wife and Vanessa forks. Everyone else hesitated briefly before Dad gave the nod of approval, then they all laughed and started digging in.

Dad and I made the rounds again as people finished eating and started cleaning up, thanking people for coming and seeing them out when they were ready. Once everyone else was gone and it was just our little group again, we pulled apart the remaining pieces of Vanessa's family's bread that they had saved. Jenny, Clarise, and Lisa made Dad promise to tell Mom that she couldn't miss any more of our get-togethers—missing this one was too much. We spent the rest of the time teasing Dad. When the parents said it was time for everyone to leave, I was sadder than I wanted to admit. The three of us hugged for a long moment again.

"Miss you already," Faye said sincerely.

"See you in a few weeks," Vanessa said. "It makes it less sad."

"Love you both for always," I promised. Dad and I left shortly after because Uncle D was closing today. I made him promise to come to a family dinner soon, and he surprised me by asking if he could bring a date. As the naturally nosy Virgo I was, I of course said yes.

"Only if I get every detail about her," I teased.

"Duh, and actually . . . them," Uncle D answered easily. I gave him a thumbs-up and a long hug goodbye.

When I sank my first hole in one on hole one, I pretended to be surprised. The yellow-and-white dress I wore with my favorite jean jacket blew in the wind as I walked to retrieve the ball. Mom had helped me roll up the cuffs of my jacket to give it a "little extra something." She was right—I did look really cute. George stood there, shocked and in awe, and then picked me up and spun me around. I put my arms out as he spun me, like I was a bird. I was grateful I'd decided to wear biker shorts underneath my dress. As I twirled, I giggled like a schoolgirl. In my defense, his excitement was contagious. I even missed the next two putts to keep him on his toes. However, by my third hole in one, I knew George had figured out my game.

"You swindled me!" he said, crossing his arms and pouting as we walked to the sixth hole. I lined up my next shot and looked over at him. He winked and then went back to pretend pouting. I took the shot and missed, this time not on purpose.

"I did no such thing. You assumed I was bad at mini golf, and you know what they say about people who assume, George Fallon." I sunk the ball on my second shot and then stepped aside so George could take his turn.

"The full name, ouch!" George laughed, before he sank a hole in one of his own. He shrugged his shoulders as if he wasn't fazed, but I saw his fist pump to himself and giggled.

"Game on!"

I had fun trash talking for the remainder of the holes. True to my word, I won the round, but it was really close and I honestly really enjoyed myself. We went out for ice cream after, where I took another victory lap, and George clapped for me even when no one else knew why. At least he was a good sport—I loved that about him. Wait, I loved that about him? The thought made my heart race. Maybe my plan was working.

We ducked out of the ice cream shop when we saw Peter, one of George's teammates, and congratulated each other on being so stealthy. I couldn't say that it didn't still hurt to be his secret, but maybe we were working to a big reveal during the new school year. Maybe this summer was just for us. He smiled and pressed me into him close enough to breathe in his cologne, which smelled like pine trees and freshly washed laundry, so there was a bit of a thrill in it. The date was truly perfect; that is, until we pulled up to my street.

Hailee was sitting on the porch.

~~~

I said goodbye to George and winced a little as he kissed my cheek.

"She doesn't look happy. Text you later," George said, and drove off when I shut the door. I waited until he was out of sight before looking up at Hailee, who stood there staring back.

"Wow, okay, cool. It's good to know that you've been ignoring me for days so you could be with George Fallon," Hailee yelled. I felt myself become angry immediately. What gave her the right to invade my space? When she kissed me and said it was a mistake! She didn't get to be upset when she had been radio silent!

"I'm not doing this here," I said through clenched teeth, walking up, my anger seeping out between my lips. I said nothing as I strode past Hailee and into my house. Hailee followed me, the door slamming louder than either of us intended.

"Mom, Dad, I'm home. Hailee and I are going upstairs," I called out before walking up the stairs without looking back. I waited until we were in my room, with the door closed, before I spoke again. There was no need for my parents to hear this.

"What are you doing here?" I asked with my hands on my hips, trying to control my breathing. I watched Hailee flinch at the question before schooling her face to reflect her anger again. I moved to my chair and sat, waiting for the answer.

"I talked to Olivia and she told me you two made up. But I guess we can't?" Hailee asked rhetorically, before pressing on. "You get a boyfriend and suddenly I'm not welcome?" She scoffed at me and studied me for a beat. I hated the way it made my stomach swoop, despite everything. "Never thought you'd be one of those girls."

"He's not my boyfriend, and last I checked you were the one who left this room after—"

"I said it was a mistake," Hailee cut in.

"OF COURSE I AM!" I yelled as I worked to dig my heartache down deep, and let the anger surge to the surface. If I was being honest, my heart—which was barely mended in the first place—had just broken into a million little pieces again. I could not let Hailee see it.

"I didn't say that," Hailee scoffed, her body recoiling at the mere suggestion. She looked at me now like I had two heads, and she wasn't sure which one to look at.

"You might as well have," I whispered. I stood and fixed her with my best glare. "I said I wasn't ready to talk. I asked you for space, Hailee."

"I'm supposed to be your best friend, and you're ignoring me to go out on dates with a boy you told me you'd stop seeing? You asked me for space, *days* after I left here in tears. You're really something, Drea," Hailee spat.

"That's not fair at all. You're the one who left me standing here crying. The one who shunned me at paintball. You ran like your feet were on fire!" I yelled back. "You don't get to act all high-and-mighty. If I'm not the mistake, then why was kissing me one?"

"Go ahead, tell me about the date. Was it everything you wanted it to be? Must've been something special. Did he . . . did he kiss you?" Hailee asked, biting her lip when I said nothing. She stepped back toward the door—she wanted to run. I could see it in her face. But I wasn't going to let her this time, so I moved to block her. I didn't miss the way she evaded my question either. Why wasn't she answering me?

"So what if he did? Why does it matter who I'm seeing, if kissing me was a mistake?" I asked. Hailee looked at me again as though I'd slapped her.

"Because I shouldn't have kissed you moments after you showed me just how little I mean to you," Hailee answered, shaking her head in shame. She put more distance between us, and though we were in the same room, she felt worlds away.

"You don't get to tell me how little or how much you mean to me," I shot back, pointing an accusing finger at her before wrapping protective arms around myself. "You don't have the right to tell me how I feel."

"I don't even care anymore. What's clear to me now is that you're a person who ditches and lies to her friends because of a high school boy who is never going to love you." Hailee folded her own arms. The room grew quiet. We were both breathing like we'd run six miles.

"You don't know anything." I swallowed, unfolding my arms and letting them fall to my side. The lump in my throat grew as Hailee laughed bitterly.

"I know the fantasy you have in your head is just that. Let's be real, he is not yours forever. We're in high school. What happens when he breaks your heart? Because he will. I have read enough books to know–"

"George really likes me and we're only keeping thing–um—secret for right now. You'll see, this is different," I fought back. I wanted Hailee to think I was confident in the future with George, but that gnawing feeling from the ice cream shop came rushing back.

"Did you ever stop to ask yourself if he's embarrassed of you, Andrea?" Hailee asked. I cringed as she stepped closer. She wasn't going to kiss me again—that much I knew—but she was close enough for me to smell her perfume, and I hated how familiar it still felt.

"Are you?" I challenged. Hailee took several steps back.

"The fact that you'd even think to ask that tells me everything I need to know. Drea, when he breaks your heart, don't come crying to me," Hailee said.

Little did she know, I was really trying not to cry right now. I stood firmly in front of the door like it was my last line of defense, clenching and unclenching my fists to distract my body from disobeying me. I didn't know who this Hailee was, but I didn't like her.

"If you don't care about my relationship, then why are you so mad? Why are you here?" I shouted, though we were close enough to hear each other.

"It's not a real relationship if no one gets to know, Andrea," Hailee said through gritted teeth.

"Whatever," I hurled back, because it was all I could manage. Hailee was really yanking at my every insecurity, and I hated how the part about it not being real felt so true.

"You ignored me for days. I couldn't eat or sleep, and you're posting on social media like nothing is wrong. I came here to see if you were sorry. It's clear you're not," Hailee said. She uncrossed her arms and matched my clenched fists.

Now we were inches away from each other, just like the day we'd kissed. This felt different—this *was* different, I reminded myself. I wasn't nervous. I was angry and hurting, and I wasn't giving in. I ran a hand through my hair and rolled my eyes.

"I'm sorry, what? You've got to be kidding me. Your heart is broken? That's rich. I won't apologize for taking a break. You forget that you stormed out of here and said nothing of substance to me for weeks! But now you hear about me with someone else and suddenly you want to talk? That's not how this works!" I was certain that my parents could hear us yelling now, but was too upset to care.

"Stop talking about that! I said I was sorry!" Hailee yelled back, her voice breaking.

"No you didn't! But I'm glad to hear it," I cut back, sarcastically. I walked past her, unblocking the door and putting more space between us. "Wouldn't want you making any more mistakes, now, would we?"

"You know what, Drea . . . I don't want to be your best friend anymore," Hailee said, angrily swiping at her face. "And there's no maybe about it. I'm done."

"I don't want to be yours. You're not much of one anyway—you can't even be happy for me. *I'm* done," I declared. I felt like my world was ending, but then I thought of George and how happy I'd been with him hours earlier. I pushed the other thoughts down. Hailee refused to break eye contact with me, but I didn't back down either. When Mom opened the door, we both jumped.

"Girls, what is happening here?" Mom asked, looking between us. Hailee turned away from me and back toward the door.

"Sorry, I was just leaving," Hailee replied, refusing now to look at me or Mom.

"Yeah," I called out, "you've gotten really good at walking away, haven't you Hails," as she closed the door.

"Andrea Monet Williams!" Mom chastised. I turned away from the door and wiped my eyes.

"Sorry Mom, our friendship is over anyway," I said, when I collected myself. She waited until we were

downstairs and sitting on the couch with my Dad before she
spoke again.

~~~

"Start from the beginning," Mom said. She grabbed my hand,
which just made me cry harder. Dad squeezed my other and I
took a steadying breath.

"I was in love with her and then we fought about George,
who I want to love, and we kissed at your anniversary party, and
then she said it was a mistake. Then we fought at the paintball
place, so I needed to take a few days and I wasn't talking to her
and now we're not friends, and I hate it, but also she was never
going to love me back and—" I rushed. I clasped my hand over
my mouth. I had just come out to my parents. "I-I mean—"

"Shh, breathe," Dad said. He grabbed the hand Mom
was already holding and squeezed it. He looked over at her
and shrugged. "E, you were right."

"What?" I asked hiccuping through my tears. I looked
between my parents and they were still gazing at each other. I
stopped hiccuping and wiped my eyes with the backs of my
hands, though it was useless because the tears just kept coming.

"What your dad is getting at"—Mom cut her husband
with a look—"is that, we thought you might've liked Hailee as
more than a friend for a while now."

"At least two years," Dad cut in, rubbing his shoulder
when Mom swatted it. "Ow."

Mom rolled her eyes and sucked her lip. "How is that
helping? Hush, let me talk," she said. I watched my parents,

dumbfounded, and even though I was really brokenhearted, right now, I felt immense relief that they weren't freaking out about the fact that I loved Hailee. Even though I was panicking about it myself. I hadn't realized that I had been in love with her for two years, but thinking back, it made sense. The longing to see her, the glances, the butterflies, and the excitement every time we sat next to each other in class, in back seats, at concerts. The nights she spent on the right side of my bed. The dreams I hid about her being the person I was walking down the aisle to, and not Manny Jacinto.

"So, you don't hate me?" I asked, my tears subsiding for the time being. I looked back down at the rug under my feet. My mind was running a mile a minute trying to figure out what to do next. How would I let my former best friend go? How to be certain my parents loved me still? How was I going to complete the list without Hailee?

"Sweetie, we love you so much. Who you fall in love with won't change that ever," Mom said. I was so relieved I jumped up to hug them. When our bodies met, we all started crying.

"Thank you, I love you guys too, so much," I blubbered into my dad's shoulder. I kissed Mom's cheek and pulled away. I felt my head and heart starting to settle, and I knew that I must look horrible. My parents were watching me again—I could feel their eyes on me. Without even having to look, I knew that there was never anything to fear, that they'd always have my back. I was so lucky.

"We were thinking of mac and cheese with meatloaf for dinner," Dad said, and I nodded enthusiastically. I loved Dad's mac and cheese with meatloaf. If anything could make me feel better, it was that. "We just need a few more things from the store."

"Can I come?" I asked.

"Please," Dad answered, kissing my forehead quickly before grabbing the car keys.

As we hit the street, I texted Fiona and Charlie.

Andrea: Having a really bad day can we hang tomorrow?

Char: We heard that you and Olivia made up and that's great. We're so happy, we love you, but the thing is

Fi: Everything with Hailee is so complicated . . .

Andrea: Come on guys, Hailee came over to my house and tore me apart. I didn't deserve that.

Fi: Drea, we told Hailee the same thing. We don't like the way either of you are behaving.

Char: You don't seem like yourself and neither does she. Hailee is hurting just as much as you are.

Andrea: So that's it? You guys are just taking Hailee's side? What happened to not choosing?

Char: We aren't choosing
Fi: We love you both but we need some space from
    you two until this is sorted. Being in the middle
    is exhausting. We just need time, okay?
Andrea: Okay.


I put down my phone and sighed.

When George asked me if I wanted to meet at the grocery store the next day, I was confused until he clarified that it was a great day for a picnic in the park. George was so nice, and even though things were terrible otherwise, I wasn't going to ignore the one thing going well to be sad about the bad. I couldn't ghost George—my mama raised me better than that. So I met him at the store thanks to Dad, who grumbled the whole way.

"I'm not trying to tell you what to do, but I prefer Hailee," he said as I got out of the car. I turned back to him and closed my eyes for a second. Letting out a breath, I cut my eyes at the car behind ours, now beeping for Dad to move. How was anyone in a rush in a grocery store parking lot? It wasn't a race. I rolled my eyes at the driver, whose hand was now firmly planted on the horn, and looked back at my dad, who shrugged as if he'd said nothing at all.

"You're not helping, Daddy," I said, before waving good-bye and going into the store. George and I met by the produce section. When we got to the park, I spotted a tree in the shade. We sat and talked as the park started to fill up with people. We made up stories about the families who passed us by. The wives with two kids getting ready for boarding school in the fall; the single dad chasing after his daughter, who he was trying to get to dance class on time; the childless couple clearly smitten with each other. We watched them for a while—they were always touching in some form or other, even when they weren't directly interacting with each other. Sure, it was a little overkill, but it was still sweet.

"Do you want kids?" George asked, looking away from the couple first. I could feel his eyes on me, but I was still watching them on the bench, their hands interlocked.

"Someday," I said, finally looking at George. "Much later in life. I want to see the world first."

"Me too," George said. He plucked a few pieces of grass out of the ground and sighed. There was definitely more to the story, and I didn't want to press too hard, but we were there to get to know each other and maybe telling me would make him feel better. A small prompting might do the trick.

"But . . ." I encouraged him. He ran a hand through his hair and let out a huff, then slid that famous smile on his face.

"Do I get something for sharing?" he asked, leaning toward me suggestively. I swatted his arm but leaned in too.

"The satisfaction of getting that heavy weight off your chest," I teased back. He threw his hands up in the air like he'd been bested by a master and laughed to let me know he was teasing.

"My parents want me to focus on soccer. They said I can travel when my professional career is over," he said. He picked at the grapes on his plate, avoiding my gaze. I didn't speak until he looked back up at me.

"I'm sorry. That is a lot of pressure. At least they believe in you?" I suggested. I knew how lucky I was to have parents who supported whatever career I wanted for myself. The amount of pressure that people like George faced seemed exhausting.

"They believe I can be their ticket to wealth," he said sadly, biting his lip. "Soccer games were the only time they didn't fight in front of me . . . other than Talia's," he laughed. "So I stuck with it. And I got good."

"You're really good, the best on your team," I added.

"And they think I can be great. So, my focus has to be on soccer one hundred and ten percent come fall. They found a club for me to join that doesn't interfere with school, and they are both so excited, I'm no longer the middle man in their arguments . . . so I'll take it," he said, unable to manage a smile this time. I reached across the blanket to grab his hand and squeezed it.

"I don't know whether to be happy for you or worried," I answered finally. He laughed, but there was no humor in it.

"You and me both," he said after a beat. He squeezed my hand back and shook his head as if to clear it, but his hair fell in front of his eyes. I released his hand to push it back for him, and a smile blossomed, twice as big as normal. "You can keep your hand in my hair—in fact, I'd prefer it—but I just heard what sounded like an earthquake rumble come from your stomach. So maybe we should eat?" I laughed so hard I snorted. He pouted when I did actually take my hand out of his hair, but he survived.

"I needed this today, thank you!" I told him. He smiled softly and moved closer on the blanket. I rolled my eyes but leaned into it. I guess he was going to be rewarded for sharing after all.

Try as I might to deny it, though, something felt off, and I couldn't shake a small thought creeping up to the front of my mind. Did I really want to be here—like *really* really? I wasn't entirely sure, but as George got closer, I told myself I should try to be in the moment.

Inches away from my face, he jumped.

"Fallon? Is that you?" a voice called out. George's eyes bugged out as he looked past me. I tried to follow his line of vision, but George scrambled to stand and gather the food. He waited impatiently while I did the same, ignoring my question about whether this was really that big of a deal. He kept looking at me and then the two people approaching us: his teammates, Jake and Sean.

"What are you doing? Go hide!" George bit out. I scoffed. He was serious. Instead of following his orders, I placed my hand on my hip incredulously.

"Hide where? Behind that thin tree or that thin tree?" I asked sarcastically, pointing to my left and my right. George, still panicked, looked from me back to his friends. From the expression on his face, he was sure to pass out from his apparent embarrassment. I guess that question about whether I really wanted to be here had been answered for me. *No*—and neither did George.

"They've already seen me," I said, visibly hurt by his behavior. He looked back over at me like I'd spilled red paint on his favorite shirt. He was just going to kiss me moments ago. Asshole. I looked away from him as the guys reached us and put space between us, crossing my arms.

"Hey man," Sean, one of the soccer team co-captains, supplied. I watched them "bro" hug. Sean and his shaggy blond hair took a while to look at me, but Jake, the tall and burly other captain beside him, zeroed in on me immediately. This was not going to go well. Jake's eyes searched between the two of us like we were a mystery to solve. I rolled my eyes, desperate for the situation to be over. A slow smile spread across Jake's face, and I began mentally preparing the comebacks I always kept loaded for ignorant white-boy jocks who thought these were the glory years and they were going to be on top forever. I let myself look over at George, who refused to return my glance. Coward.

"Well, well, what do we have here?" Jake asked, standing on the picnic blanket, closer to George.

"Nothing," George said quickly. I was already planning my exit. I reached down to grab the grocery bag and put my unopened chips and drink in. When I placed it on my arm and stood back up, I looked over at Sean, who had the grace to at least look embarrassed. I slid my gaze back over to Jake, who had the slyest smile on his thin lips. I steeled myself for whatever was coming next.

"Seriously dude, what is this? Like, Make-A-Wish? Take-a-cripple-on-a-date contest?" He laughed, while the other two looked horrified.

"Dude!" Sean called out. I looked over at George, who found his shoes too interesting to defend me. So, I was going at this alone, cool. This wouldn't be the first or the last time. I nodded my head in understanding. I turned my attention back to Jake, who was looking at me like I was going to crumble, but I'd heard worse. In fact, he caught me on the right day. I cracked my neck and began.

"Make-A-Wish, right? Haha, good one. You should probably make a wish that your hairline stops receding between now and graduation day," I launched in. I watched him touch his hairline self-consciously and pressed on. "That's the best you've got? Make-A-Wish and cripple? Is that truly the best you've got? Because here's what I know to be true, Jake: you're a coward who cried when I refused to tutor you in history . . . you know, the class we shared because you failed like two years in a row? Do you not remember how much you needed this cripple then? Anyway, let's move on to the fact that no matter how much body spray you wear, you will never get rid of that BO your mom probably tells you everyone has so you don't cry to her about it. And long after this 'cripple' leaves this town, you'll still be here trying to fit into your varsity jacket, while your poor wife wishes she married literally anyone else."

I smiled, knowing I'd gotten under his skin, as Jake stood there with his mouth slightly open. I pushed past the three of them.

"Andrea," George called out to me. I turned around and cut him with a glare.

"Don't worry, I'm leaving. You and me? That's done. Lose my number," I said. I walked away as his friends giggled in response. When I was out of sight, I called Charlie. As the phone rang, I looked around me at the joy on the other people's faces as they passed by. I felt sick. How could I have been so stupid? I felt nothing but anger and embarrassment for going out with him in the first place.

"Hello?" Charlie said, snapping me back to the issue at hand. I swallowed and stepped aside to let a family walk by.

"I know you and Fi need space, but could you come get me from the park? I'll explain when you get here," I rushed out, and found that my face was wet.

"Okay . . . are you crying?" Charlie asked.

"No," I said, though I had already sniffled on the phone. I was so tired of crying. I wiped my eyes sloppily and turned the other direction.

"We're on our way, Andie," Charlie said. I think she had put me on speaker. They only called me Andie when they were worried, so I knew she'd heard me crying now. I was still so relieved that I stepped back out from behind the tree I was hiding behind.

"Meet us at the entrance of the park," Fiona said. I thanked them and ended the call.

My legs began to sting as I made my way up the hill and through the park toward the entrance. I couldn't stop though—I had to push through. When I saw the bench at the park's entrance, I sighed in relief. I did feel guilty about calling Fiona and Charlie, but I couldn't deal with how my parents would react. At least this way I could calm down on the way home and figure out how to tell them everything—and keep them from finding Jake's parents and telling them about their son and themselves. It's not like we lived in a world where Black people could do that sort of thing without a cop being called, and without my parents being painted as the aggressors—even though they'd just be using their words. Money couldn't save us from that.

Fiona pulled up and honked a few minutes later. I rubbed my knee quickly and got in the back seat. I put my seat belt on and sighed. I was doing that way too much as well. Charlie turned around and squeezed my hand. I smiled, lightly, grateful for the contact and for both of them. Fiona didn't move the car yet, but she kept her eyes forward. I let go of Charlie's hand and looked down at the mats on the floor. I knew I needed to fix things with them first.

"What happened?" Charlie asked, still looking at me intently. She cleared her throat when I didn't respond, and I stopped staring at the corner of the floor mat and looked back up at her. The truth was that I was so embarrassed, I almost wanted to lie to save myself. But look where that had gotten me before: friendless and heartbroken. The exact place I never wanted to be again. I was determined to tell the truth only from now on.

"George and I came here for a picnic in the park, and everything was fine, until his friends showed up," I said. Charlie turned back around and put on her seat belt, but signaled for me to continue. Fiona pulled out of the parking lot and onto the road. "He was angry because I refused to hide, but they'd already seen me and came over to say hi, and then Jake called me a cripple and asked if our date was a Make-A-Wish thing."

"Are you fucking kidding me?" Fiona said, swerving back into the parking lot. It was really nice to hear her voice. "Is he still here? I'll punch him." Fiona circled the lot, and I realized just how good I had it. I loved my friends so much. I leaned forward and told Fiona he wasn't worth it. Fiona pulled back out to head home, but muttered the rest of the way.

"What did George say to defend you?" Charlie asked. I laughed humorlessly and looked down at my shoes. In what was a surprise even to me, this was the part that hurt worse than the names Jake had called me. For George to stand there quietly while his friend said those terrible things to the girl he claimed to like was the most disgusting part. The thing was, I already knew Jake was pathetic, and he in no way impacted how I saw myself. But the fact that George stayed silent?

"Nothing," I said, finally. Charlie blew out a breath, reaching her arm back and offering her hand once more. I slid mine to hers easily; she squeezed it three times. I loved her back. I listened to the low hum of the radio, not interested in singing along. We were well past the park when Fiona said what we were all thinking.

"Prick."

My sentiments exactly.

"Forget about them. I have just the song to turn this ride around," Fiona announced. I laughed as "He Wasn't Man Enough" by Toni Braxton pumped out from her phone through the speakers moments later.

We spent the rest of the ride home singing songs at the top of our lungs and laughing when no one could hold the high notes. By the time we reached my street, I'd almost forgotten why I was upset in the first place. As Fiona pulled into my driveway, I undid my seat belt and hugged them both the best I could. I promised to give them the space they deserved and got out of the car. We exchanged "I love yous" and I watched them peel off and turned toward my front door.

There was no more avoiding the inevitable. I groaned and walked inside. I took off my shoes and padded my way to the living room to find my parents cuddled up on the couch. I cleared my throat to let them know I was coming, then walked past them to put my drink in the fridge. I pulled the chips out of the bag and opened them.

"Hey baby, how was your date?" Mom asked, watching me. I walked over to the couch and sat beside my mother. My parents were watching the Food Network. I ate a few more chips before looking over at them both.

"Horrible. Fiona and Charlie dropped me home," I said, as the person on TV put the mac and cheese in the pre-heated oven. Dad paused the TV and put the remote down. I cracked my neck and scratched the itch on my nose. They were going to want to hear the whole story, but I had to choose my words wisely. My parents were reactors, and I was an only child—they reacted quickly. I didn't want them flying off the handle, though it was nice to know they were always ready and willing.

"George and I were having a nice lunch until his friends came over. George wanted me to hide but there was nowhere to go and—"

"He wanted my baby to hide?" Dad cut in. "Like he's embarrassed of her? Absolutely not." He moved to stand, but Mom and I put a hand on his arm to stop him.

"Let her finish, D. Dang," Mom said, rolling her eyes before she gestured for me to continue. My dad, to his credit, sat back down in a huff. I reached over and patted his shoul-der reassuringly.

"Anyway, his friends came over and one of them insinuated that George was doing a Make-A-Wish date with me, which makes no sense considering. Then his friend called me a cripple, I ripped him a new one, and then I left." I held my breath.

"What did George say to defend you?" Mom asked. She was carrying her anger in her raised eyebrow.

"Nothing. He said nothing," I answered, my initial anger and hurt resurfacing. I balled my fists up and squeezed them before releasing and letting my anger go with them.

"I told you I didn't like that little boy, did I not?" Dad said to Mom, who scoffed and put a single finger up in the air.

"This is not about you, D," she replied, imploring him to remain focused. "Your daughter was just humiliated. No one cares if you were right."

"I wouldn't say humiliated. I handled my own," I said back, and as I did, I realized how proud I was for immediately sticking up for myself and not waiting for a defense that wouldn't come. The more I thought about it, the more I understood that I didn't need George to love me or defend me—I needed to do it myself, and I would.

"Of course you did, you are my daughter," Mom said, flipping her hair. I laughed and stood up. After reassuring them that I was fine, I kissed both of their cheeks and told them I was going to my room, giving them a thumbs-up that I knew they still thought was cool. But rather than head upstairs when I left, what I actually did was duck behind the living room wall, so I could hear what they were really thinking. I knew my parents well enough to know that they had been holding back.

"So, for a moment there, you wished you were that kid's age so you could beat him up too, right?" Dad whispered to Mom.

"Absolutely. But what I really want is for him to get the runs every time something important happens for the rest of his life," she countered. I snickered and shook my head. George would deserve that. There was silence for a few moments, and I debated walking away, thinking the conversation was over. But then, "I will be talking to his mother and telling her about her son and herself. What Drea doesn't know won't hurt her," Mom said. I rolled my eyes from where I stood, but I knew she wouldn't overdo it.

"I'm proud of her. Maybe you can get out of her what she said specifically, later? I'm nosy," Dad reminded Mom, as if either of us could forget.

"I'll tell you both at dinner," I called out, laughing and heading up the stairs.

"Want to come to New York City with me tomorrow? Just me and you, a girls' weekend. Might do you some good to get away for a while?" Mom asked. Her hands playfully clasped in front of her like she wasn't opposed to begging. I giggled at the thought.

"Yes please!"

"Great! And by the way, I'm really glad you and Olivia made up. You know, it's not too late to make up with Hailee too." Mom smiled at me and unclasped her hands. She bopped my nose. Maybe she was right.

~~~

For all the teasing Mom gave Dad about his need to be extremely early everywhere, we were definitely at the airport way too early. Mom thought our one o'clock flight was at eleven in the morning, and she didn't want to leave and come back, or try to get an earlier flight. So instead we sat at our gate with breakfast sandwiches and large drinks, with more than enough time to use the bathroom.

Mom switched between her phone and her computer, typing out emails and approving or vetoing design and fabric requests.

"Olivia says she hopes we have a safe flight," Mom said. We both smiled at each other. "It's nice to text her again."

"Tell her thank you! And I'm glad you get to now, too."

I texted Faye and Vanessa. Faye was getting ready for her community theater audition. She still wouldn't tell us what the play was because she loved a surprise. She did snap a pic of the theater's entry doors, though it provided no clues. Vanessa was at the stables, getting ready to go riding on her horse, Cassie. Vanessa had always loved horses, and the fact that she was able to ride with her moms as her side walkers was her dream come true. She sent a picture of her and Cassie side-by-side, her wide smile making me smile through the phone. I made Mom lean in for a picture of us at the gate.

Nessa: Have fun in NYC. Let it take your mind off of everything.

Fayelala: If you go see a show, bring me back a Playbill. We love you!

Andrea: Give Cassie and the theater my love. Love you too!

"So, I was thinking—" Mom ended her phone call and turned toward me. I stopped my music and took out my head-phones to give her my full attention. "Once we get to the city, we can drop our bags off, head to the store for a bit, and then come back and order room service?"

"Yes please." I was smiling so hard my cheeks should've hurt.

~~~

Once we landed, and had gone to the hotel and dropped off all our bags, we stopped by a park for some fresh air. We watched a family walking past us: a mom, a father, and a little girl. I wondered if Mom was missing Dad. The little girl waved at me, and I gave her a small smile, waving back.

"I remember when you were that little. You were so excited by everything," Mom said. She wasn't wrong. When I was the same age as that little girl and we visited the city, my parents would let me hang from their arms like I was weightless, flying, my feet barely touching the ground until we reached the baggage carousel to see Grandpa Sam standing there, his arms outstretched for me. I would take off running each time, closing the distance as matching smiles spread across our faces and he called me His Favor-ite Girl. We always made a park our first stop. Even as I got older, he kept the endearing name, and I kept running to him, careful to be gentle as I watched him grow older. See-ing that little girl reminded me just how much I missed him still.

"Ready to go to work?" Mom asked, pulling me back to her.

"Sounds great," I said, biting my lip. "But Mom, before I say what I'm about to say, I need you to promise not to overreact." We rounded the corner a couple blocks away from the store. She arched an eyebrow, but I pressed on.

"What am I not overreacting to?" Mom laughed, adjusting the strap of her purse on her shoulder.

"This is some of the most fun I've had all summer. I love you, Mommy. Thank you," I said casually. I fought the laughter for as long as I could, but when she pulled me into a hug and swung us around once, I couldn't contain it anymore. She kissed my forehead after she let me go.

"That's you not overreacting?" I teased. Mom shrugged and looked away from me, a smile on her lips.

"I never agreed not to overreact, in my defense. I just asked what you were going to make me not overreact to. I love being here with you too, Drea." Mom flipped her hair behind her shoulder like she was at the end of a runway, looking over at me to see if she had a captive audience. She always would. She nudged her shoulder against mine, and we picked our walking pace back up.

My phone buzzed in my pocket and I pulled it out to look.

G: I made a mistake. Please respond. Look, I'm
    under a lot of pressure at school and my friends

expect certain things from me. I really like you and I told them not to say anything so we can still hang out.

I stopped walking to type. Walking and texting was harder than it looked.

> Andrea: Congrats on having friends who will keep your secret. But the thing is, I don't want to be your secret. I deserve the real thing. I was never going to have that with you.
>
> G: That's not fair you said you were fine with keeping this between us. Now you're changing your mind because my friends made stupid little comments. He was just joking. I'll make him apologize.
>
> Andrea: I realize I deserve more than that. I don't need or want his apology. I needed you to defend me.

Mom offered me her outstretched hand and I squeezed it once quickly before stepping inside.

~~~

"Monet!" Fredrick called out when they saw me. I looked around my mother's flagship store. I knew my mother worked hard—there was no way we would have what we did if she didn't—but seeing the inside of her store was a different story.

I heard gasps from some of the customers as she walked in, like they couldn't believe their eyes. Sometimes I couldn't believe mine either. All around me were floor-to-ceiling windows, flanked by impeccably dressed mannequins in a mix of streetwear and rock-inspired clothing, with more feminine and bright-colored pieces slid in there making everything feel and look high-end. The mix of designs shouldn't work so well with each other but they did somehow. And from the look of it, business was booming. Mom said hello to the customers and I left her as she stepped behind the counter to help cash people out and visit with them.

"Freddie P!" I called back, giving Fredrick my best model walk as I made my way over to them. They clapped for me when my runway ended, and we went downstairs where everyone was hard at work.

"How are you?" I asked. They smiled back as they maneuvered between the open-concept office desks, vetoing ideas and approving the ones that fit the brand best. Their jet-black, curly hair was pulled into a ponytail and the crisp black-and-white suit they wore was a sample Mom had designed in hopes of adding a menswear line to the Evelyn Williams brand, which I affectionately referred to as the EWFU (Evelyn Williams Fashion Universe). One of these days it was going to catch on.

"I'm tired, Mo. Tired but happy. Doing what I love," they said easily. "Let's go to my office. I have some things I want to run by you." I nodded and we began walking toward the back. I waved hello to a few of the employees I recognized and followed Fredrick into their glass office. The floor plan was supposed to make everyone feel like they were a part of a team and a family. Still, Mom and Fredrick had their own actual offices and a privacy button that allowed them to speak or move around without anyone hearing or seeing inside. Neither really used it. I sat down on the comfiest couch ever. I had no idea black leather could feel like a cloud, but here we were. My butt and my knees were grateful for the rest.

"How are you, Monet?" they asked me, expecting honesty. If Uncle D was my dad's brother in every way but blood, Fredrick was my mom's sibling just the same. They had this thing about not calling me by my first name, because they gave me my middle name and felt it suited me better. I was strictly forbidden to call them "Uncle," but every year on my birthday and Christmas I got extravagant gifts my mom couldn't send back . . . so, I got over it.

I shrugged. "Life sucks right now to be honest." They smiled at me like they knew something I didn't and pulled some papers from the desk of their drawer.

"I remember being your age," they said, looking off to the side, caught in a memory. "It was only four years ago."

I laughed, grateful for the levity. "Four? I thought it was two?"

"Good girl," they praised me, the laugh sparkling in their eyes. I really didn't get to see Fredrick enough. It sucked.

This was already improving my mood and an hour hadn't even passed. "Want to take some of it off your shoulders?"

"Well, I came out to my parents—they took it well—I finally made up with my sworn enemy but Hailee and I aren't speaking, I sort of dumped the guy I was seeing because his friend called me a cripple and he said nothing, but I'm not too sad because I only dated him so I'd stop being in love with my best friend."

"Whew, that's a lot." Fredrick lined the pages neatly and motioned for me to move closer, so I did.

"There's more: she kissed me and then said it was a mistake. Now we aren't friends anymore."

"A mistake? That's harsh."

"I know, and I'm sad, and angry, and hurt, and—" I started, pressing my hands into the couch.

"And you miss her." Fredrick said matter-of-factly. I chewed on my lip for a moment, looking away from them and back out to the people engrossed in the work and the art of designing clothes. I was still struggling with my art, and watching everyone so focused when I couldn't be made me squirm in my seat. Fredrick cleared their throat, and I turned back to them.

"Sorry, yeah, I do . . . so much," I said, relieved to say it out loud to someone else. A knowing smile played at Fredrick's lips.

"Been there. It's hard stuff. Your mom and dad are the ones who can give you the seamless life-lesson speeches. But

I can tell you that you deserve someone who will stand up for you when need be, and someone who doesn't kiss you and call it a mistake—"

"Thank you, I—"

"But you also shouldn't date someone in order to get over someone else, that's not fair to anyone involved. I'm saying all of this out of love. I know you're hurting, and I hate that you are, but the things you're telling me don't sound like the fierce, compassionate, and kind young woman I know you to be," Fredrick finished. I hung my head for a moment. They were right—I had done things I wasn't proud of: yelling at Olivia, lying to Hailee and my parents, putting Charlie and Fiona in an awkward position. Now I had to face the consequences of my actions. It sounded like torture.

"I know, I made a lot of mistakes," I said finally, pulling the invisible lint off of my black jeans.

"It's not too late to fix them. I know you can and I know you will. But for now, I have just the thing that will cheer you up."

"What?" I said with a smile, peering over the papers in front of me.

"Samples! Want to help me decide what we love and what we don't?" Fredrick asked, even though we both knew the answer.

"Duh!" I cheered. I loved when I was given permission to take a peek at what was coming. I grabbed the clothes they brought out, laying them flat across Fredrick's desk and running my hand over my chin thoughtfully. Before me sat an array of colors, patterns, and accessories. I slid a sample of a brown chunky belt over a white dress, then paired dark-wash, flared jeans with a long sleeve yellow sweater and a set of bracelets. I took the black-and-white namesake belt and put it next to white cargo pants and a namesake crop top. Fredrick looked on approvingly. Satisfied, I sat back and awaited my evaluation.

"I'd switch the yellow sweater out and put this here," they said, replacing the sweater with a long, denim jacket over a soft, white, transparent tee. "Love the cargo and the crop. The white dress has been done too many times, but I see where you're going with this."

"So, not bad?"

"Not at all. Ev would be proud," Fredrick said easily. "If the whole art thing evolves into you wanting to work in fashion design, let me know."

"I already tried that. She's not budging; no interest in the family business," Mom said, entering the office with a laugh. She walked over to me and kissed my forehead, then moved to examine the samples more closely.

"I have what you two don't," Fredrick teased.

"And what's that?" Mom asked, shaking her head yes or no as Fredrick pulled out more samples for her to see. Fredrick looked at me conspiratorially as they switched out an option.

"Subtlety," they said simply, which made us all laugh out loud.

"Subtlety is my middle name, thank you very much. Isn't that right, baby?" Mom asked, and I avoided her gaze in favor of the black specks on the corner of my shoe.

"Between you wanting me to work in fashion and Dad telling me culinary school is the best second option, not so sure subtlety is possible for either of you," I answered, looking back up at her and trying not to laugh as she pretended to pout. Mom and Freddie P worked for another two hours, but the time flew by. I was so excited they were letting me take a few pictures for my socials—as long as they didn't show any secret info—that I didn't mind sitting around. I modeled some actual samples in the process of being mass-produced and was listened to when I said the button choices on a jacket were atrocious. Fredrick laughed at that and fixed Mom with a "told you so" look. We left their office after I made them promise to come visit with their new partner since we had more than enough room.

"Are you ready to go?" Mom asked thirty minutes later, rounding the desk in her office and making her way back toward me. I smiled at her and stood. She put her privacy screen back down and we walked back through the downstairs and the store saying our goodbyes.

"This was a fun trip, right?" Mom asked as she ordered two hot dogs on the street the next afternoon. She paid quickly and took a big bite of one when the vendor handed her both. I grabbed the other and stepped to the side to let two young Black women in their twenties pass. They both had natural hair—one in twists and the other in braids—and were kissing each other every few steps.

"I love your work," called the one wearing Mom's signature jean jacket with a pair of white jeans. The other was wearing a bright yellow dress and white Keds. They were both gorgeous.

"Thank you," Mom called back. I watched them smile excitedly at each other. I felt something bloom in my chest. It was quick and sharp, but I didn't mind it. It was hope. I watched them until they blended into the crowd, out of view. I looked over at Mom who I realized had done the same.

"That could be you one day," Mom leaned over conspiratorially, smiling at my hitch of breath. "I hope I like the person you'll spend your life with, Andrea. But whoever it is, know that as long as they are good to you, I'll be in their corner too."

I finally bit my hot dog for a distraction; it really was delicious. We finished them off and began walking toward a park bench, which was great because my body was starting a dull ache—a signal that I had mere minutes before it threw a tantrum.

We watched quite a few more people before we decided to leave the bench. Mom wanted to make sure that I was fully rested, and I was grateful. Every time I saw a group of what looked like friends, my heart lurched.

"Ready for the next part of today?" Mom asked excitedly, taking my hand and pulling me off the bench and back toward the street. She let my hand go to hail a cab, which stopped in seconds, like they did in the movies. She let me climb into the cab first and rattled off an address I didn't recognize as she clambered in beside me. When we pulled up to an alleyway I raised an eyebrow at her, but her smile never faltered. Mom paid and we got out. She pointed me to a side door and there was someone waiting to let us in. The hat on his head read Life's Paint Palace.

"Follow me," he said with a smile, leading us through a hallway and past room after room of people wearing painter's smocks, their work out of view. I didn't even know what this was and I loved it already. Patrick was the name of the man walking us to our room—I'd learned it as he and Mom were making conversation about true-crime documentaries. She really could befriend anyone. He steered us to a room that had two large easels with balloons taped to blank canvases. To the left of us sat smocks we put on to protect our clothes. As Mom finished tying up the strings on my smock, Patrick explained the safety protocols. We were only to aim the pins at the balloons, and not each other, only the person over eighteen could fill the new balloons and tape them up . . . yada yada yada. I was listening, I swear I was, but I was so ready to pop some balloons. Mom stood beside me in her power stance, her pin at the ready. A mischievous smile was spread across her face. Patrick backed away jokingly. "Okay you two, have fun."

"Can I do the honors?" Mom asked, once he was out of the room.

"Yes, please!" I encouraged her, snapping a picture of our set-up. Mom popped the first balloon, a yellow one with green paint inside. Mom reached for a paintbrush to swirl the color a little. She laughed loudly, like she had just heard the best joke. A smile didn't leave her face as her freckles shone in the light. Then, she paused, her chin lowered and her expression suddenly pensive. I tapped her shoulder and she turned, as if surprised to find me there.

"Looks great, Mom," I said sincerely, tucking my hair behind my ears and thinking through my own plan of attack. I made my decision, my pin ready to pierce a balloon, then realized I couldn't ignore the energy shift in the room. Something was up with my Mom, and it was my job to figure it out. I turned to her once more with what I hoped was my most convincing smile. "I mean it, you're a natural!"

"Sweetie, you know I'm not good at this stuff," she said with a hollow laugh. Was that why she never wanted to paint with me or Janice—because she thought she had to be good at it? I knew her standards were high for her work, but they weren't supposed to be high here. We were here to have fun, maybe blow off some steam. I had to stop her train of thought before it really got going.

"I'm serious. I really do like it. But there's no pressure here; this is just for fun," I promised, bumping her shoulder so she knew I meant it.

"Thank you, sweetie. I just got caught up in a memory of my mother too, but you're right. This is for fun, and I'm having the time of my life with you."

The fact that her mother was still able to make her feel like perfection was the only option made me angry. And though I wanted to ask her more about what she got caught in, I didn't want to ruin this moment.

"How could you not?" My lips curled into a smile as I dodged her swatting hand. Ah, there she was . . . I was glad I was able to pull her back.

A few hours later we were cleaned up and headed to the airport. And though our trip was over, I felt like I might just be okay after all.

As we made it home and walked inside our house, I finished telling Mom the rest of how my conversation with Olivia went. She wanted every detail. We went through the hallway and I let myself look at the photos on the wall. Mom stopped us both in front of one of them, wrapping her arm around my shoulders as I shared the last of the retelling. She nodded her head in open approval before speaking.

"On our third date, your father said something that really stuck with me. I was still really sad about my parents . . . they refused to talk to me after I moved to New York to model. He said: 'We are made up of the people we love and the people who love us in return.'" Mom patted my shoulder and left me there, still staring at the wall.

At my happiest, I looked like the picture before me, a picture of part of my family. Hailee, Janice, my parents, and I were standing in Janice's backyard after a really delicious barbecue. Faye and Vanessa had left first to beat traffic, and Fiona, Charlie, their parents, and Olivia a few hours after. There was a version of this photo in the living room with the others Photoshopped in that we all loved. In both, I wore a smile that took up my face. That was how I always smiled when I was truly happy—that was who I was. I thought about the brief for the showcase this year and the words "Show Us Who You Are," as clear in my mind as they'd ever been. I had been approaching this portrait all wrong. I dragged my suitcase up the stairs and to my room, setting my phone down. I let shuffle cure me from any post-trip sadness as I unpacked and put the clothes in my laundry. When I was done with the last of them, my phone buzzed.

Olivia: Hey, Drea?

Andrea: Yeah?

Olivia: Jamie told me about George and his idiot
    friends. Jamie ended his friendship with them.
    You know that you're beautiful just the way you
    are right?

Andrea: Yeah, I know. Thanks, Liv.

Olivia: Good. He's a coward and he never deserved
    you. Hailee does.

Andrea: Fingers crossed that I can fix this.

Olivia: Omg, the concert is canceled!

Andrea: What?

Olivia: Yeah. Hold on, I'll text the group.

A second later a text message from Gardenia's Greatest Gifts popped up.

Olivia: The Lizzo concert has been canceled 😞 :( :(

Fi: I saw. I hate it here

Char: Anyone know why?

Andrea: Scheduling conflicts according to the
internet

Fi: Let's go to the lake house early

Char: Mom and dad just said yes.

Andrea: I'm in

Hailee: Me too

Olivia: Perfect, me too. See y'all soon.

I smiled and put my phone down. Everyone was in . . . even Hailee. That part made me nervous. What would the trip be like now? She had been right about George after all. Did the girls tell her about it? Maybe, a miracle could happen, and we could make up so the summer wasn't totally ruined?

I wasn't counting on it.

~~~

An hour later, my phone buzzed in my pocket as I sat with paint on my forehead, working away at the new portrait outside.

The new direction I was going in made me so excited—not only for the showcase, but for my future. The weeks I'd spent struggling to make sense of who I was and what I wanted to paint all felt worth it now, and I wasn't even done.

I pulled my phone out of my pocket and saw texts from George and Olivia. I decided to deal with him first.

G: So that's it? You're just done?

Andrea: I want to do this in person. I want to end this in person.

G: I don't. You want me to say sorry for not defending you, but I don't know what you wanted me to say. I didn't know they'd be there.

Andrea: That's the thing, you think the problem is that they were there, but the problem is that you said nothing. If it happened again, what would you say?

G: That's unfair. I don't know. I'm not going to give up my friends.

Andrea: I'm sorry George but that's not what I need to hear. And honestly, I haven't been fair to you because my heart wasn't fully in this to begin with. You don't deserve that in the same way I don't deserve someone who can't stick up for me.

G: So we're done.

Andrea: Yeah.

G: Yeah.

I blew out a breath and switched to Olivia's messages.

Olivia: Saw this and thought of you!

I laughed at the attached GIF of a pie-eating contest that was just people plopping face first into the pies. I smiled and typed out my response.

Andrea: Where'd you find this picture of me?
Olivia: Mama Ev sent it to me a couple minutes ago
        lmao

I sent back a GIF of an infomercial where a woman dressed in business clothes, who looked a little like Olivia, spilled spaghetti on herself on purpose.

Andrea: Okay, but this one looks just like you, Liv
Olivia: I taught her everything she knows obvs.

I put my phone away and started to shape my face. I gave myself Dad's eyebrows. I kept my hair in loose curls, the way I liked it best whenever Mom helped me with it, but I added a few red streaks the same color as Faye's hair. I shaped my ears like Charlie's and my nose like Fiona's. I decided to give myself a few freckles at the start of my cheekbones, just like Mom. I borrowed the small scar on the left of my cheek from

Janice. I kept my eyes their natural color, but shaped them like Olivia's.

Vanessa had a small heart-shaped birthmark on her neck that I loved, so I added that too. I gave myself the smile I had in the picture in the foyer and Hailee's beauty mark on the right side of her chin. My left hand was a ring with purple and pink flowers to symbolize the socks Hailee and I both shared. Uncle Dennis and Fredrick took me a few minutes to think through, but then I remembered they both had their ears pierced, so I added in an earring. I toyed around with the neutral colors I was using to create my own face. I was excited to draw my Black face and my Black body, the joy radiating off the painting and onto me. Today, I didn't need the sun; I was my own light.

Finally, when I moved on to my right arm and hand, I didn't shy away from the scars or bruises. I let the way my fingers bent catch the light, no longer afraid to let my right hand be in the spotlight. George and his friends couldn't keep me from loving every part of me. The portrait version of me was sitting, because a big part of my life was about the necessity of rest. As I worked, it became clear that all of these things I was uncertain about were actually beautiful with the right mindset, light, and paint.

~~~

I put the brush down, excited that the portrait was finally done. I set everything to the side and turned off my music. Inside, my parents were watching TV and I joined them, putting my head on Mom's shoulder.

"I was thinking that maybe you and the girls would want to walk in the show during Fashion Week?" Mom asked after a while, a smile in her voice. I choked on my own spit. Mom patted my back and laughed a little. I couldn't blame her—I was actively freaking out. Walking at Fashion Week? Me? Well, I'd be limping down the runway, but that was even better! I jumped up to hug Mom, who was still sitting. I laughed into her shoulder and then pulled back. She cleared her throat all businesslike, and straightened an invisible tie.

"OMG, Mommmmmm yes! OMG the girls are going to freak! Do you think Hailee will want to? Do you think we'll be talking by then? Me, on a runway at Fashion Week! OMG! Mom! Do you think I'll belong there? Wow!" I was filled with so much energy and excitement at the idea that I could not contain it. With her hands on either arm, she smiled down at me.

"I've already asked every parent and they said okay. But they want to tell their girls themselves. Faye and Vanessa's moms said yes to the runway and a site feature. And . . . hell yes you belong on that runway with your friends! Yes," Mom said. The phone dinged with the sound of a triangle, my special text tone for the group chat with Faye and Vanessa. I picked the phone up from the couch.

Nessa: Blink twice if you're basically a supermodel
now

Andrea: My supermodel queens!

Nessa: Going to do Naomi Campbell proud!

Andrea: That's right!

Fayelala: Hey! Me too! It will be great!

Andrea: Lots to catch you two up on btw

Nessa: Spill

Andrea: George is done. That's over. He let
his friend call me cripple. Said nothing to
defend me.

Fayelala: Typical. Was anyone rooting for him?

Nessa: Not me. You let him have it, yes?

Andrea: I am my Mother's Daughter

I attached a GIF of a hair flip. I laughed out loud in the
quiet of the house and thanked my friends for making me feel
better, though they could not hear it.

Fayelala: . . . what about Hailee?

Andrea: I'm miserable without her

Nessa: Does she know this?

Andrea: I'm working on telling her.

"That's them," I announced, kissing Mom's cheek and grabbing my bags. Mom stood and walked me to the door like she was gearing up to send me off to war.

"Final check: Tiger Balm, ice pack, gel insoles for your sneakers, first aid kit? Snacks?" she asked. I rolled my eyes and smiled at her. She was adorable, even if it was a little annoying. I was seventeen after all, not nine.

"I'm going for three days, not three weeks, Mom," I said, opening the front door.

"Don't play with me. Check them off," Mom insisted, her hand on her hip, but a smile at the edge of her lips.

"Check, check, check, they have a kit at the house already. I love you, Mom. They're waiting," I said. I hugged my mom again quickly and took off down the steps and toward the

Perez's SUV. Mr. and Mrs. Perez sat in the front, Charlie, Fiona, and Olivia in the far back, while Hailee sat in one of the two seats in front of them, leaving the other open for me. I took a deep breath. But first: I walked over to the rear passenger side and knocked on the door with my left hand. Olivia pulled back in surprise when she saw what I was holding. I was so excited that I got to see that look. She took her seat belt off and jumped out of the car. I couldn't stop the smile that spread across my own face.

"So, you *did* make one for me?" Olivia asked, taking the painting out of my hand to look at it closely. She ran her fingers down the edges of the canvas. I'd used purple and blue—Olivia's favorite colors from when we were kids—to make the sky, and green for the grass. On the ground sat a little girl, in a field of daisies, sitting cross-legged in her jean shorts and a white shirt with a dancing ballerina on it. Her blond hair was in pigtail braids, her blue eyes bright, and her smile brighter.

"Believe me or not, but I did yours first. I was just too scared to give it to you," I said.

"I remember this day. It was one of the best days of my life. Remember we got lost on the way back from the kids museum and you spotted the daisies and made your parents pull over?" she asked, the smile in her voice returning.

"Yeah, my dad had just gotten that brand-new camera. But my mom took all the pictures." We laughed. Olivia didn't look away from the painting, which gave me a chance to watch her. Now that she had the painting, I wondered why I had been so nervous to give it to her. Even after our falling out, I'd thought of the day with the daisies all the time—how happy Olivia had been, but also, how happy we had been together as a family, and to have Olivia with us.

"Your mom says she still has the pictures of you and me and the ones of the four of us. Does she really?" Olivia asked, hopeful. I nodded. After Olivia and I made up, Mom put them back on the mantle. She said she had her girls back. We passed them now every time we came and went from the house. I liked knowing she was right, that we were back—and hopefully, better than ever.

Olivia walked over to the trunk and put the painting in. We hugged quickly once more as I climbed in, then Mr. Perez pulled off.

"Chip?" Hailee offered me. I was startled at her casualness. I watched her face for a moment as she held the chip between her thumb and forefinger. She wouldn't give me a poisoned chip or anything, but the offer left me a little on edge. What did this offering mean? Was she just trying to be normal again? Still, I was hungry, so I smiled and accepted it. I turned around in my seat as best I could with my seat belt on and waved at Charlie and Fiona.

"This is going to be the best weekend," Charlie announced, leaning forward for emphasis.

"Let's get a picture, it's been a minute," Hailee said, and every one of us leaned in to make sure we were all in the frame. We took two pictures and went back to singing. I pulled out my phone and took a picture of the trees as we passed them. I decided then that my next project would be to capture nature as I encountered it in my everyday life.

> @HaileeTxo: The boys are back in town ♫ @OhCharlie @FiThatsMe @OliviaHope @DreaWArt

Hailee attached the picture and showed us all before posting.

We arrived at the lake house in record time. Hailee wordlessly grabbed my bag for me and headed inside, followed quickly by Fiona and Charlie and their parents. I stood for a moment admiring the shade of green the Perezes had chosen for the outside, though the entire house was breathtaking. There were freshly cut shrubs surrounding the front, with planters designed for the windows, and the attached garage door opened to reveal a row of bikes for each of the family. My favorite thing, though, was the grassy path that led the way to their dock where their boat and Jet Skis were ported. Back toward the entrance of the house where I stood now was a stone walkway, leading to a porch swing that I'd definitely find time to sit on later. Olivia bounced over to my right side and took my arm, pulling me out of my thoughts.

"I think you're going to leave this weekend a completely different person," she said cryptically. She smiled at me and switched her bag to her other shoulder. I looked at her and scrunched my nose the way we used to when we were younger and couldn't figure out what was going on. Olivia played along and tapped her nose twice, which was a signal to me that I needed to concentrate. The thing was, I didn't know what I was supposed to be concentrating on.

"What does that mean?" I asked. Olivia just smiled as we walked toward the door.

"You'll see," she said, as we stepped inside.

I loved the Perezes' lake house for the same reason I loved Hailee's house: it was cozy. I was obsessed with spaces that felt lived-in, homey. Sure, I had a lot of comfortable spaces in my home, spaces that I loved, but my parents weren't fans of the kind of clutter that made certain homes feel like a warm blanket on a cold day. They liked sleekness and open concepts; modern design and neutral colors.

The Perezes had at least one vibrant color in every room, but they all worked so well together. Everyone sat in the living room with their bags piled together in the center. Olivia was on one side of me and Hailee on the other. I'd never thought I'd see this day again. Charlie, Fiona, and their parents sat on the couch across from us. I let my head fall back against the couch as I laughed at the story being told, one about the time Charlie stuck bath beads up her nose and smelled like lavender for a week.

"Remember the first time Andrea went tubing? She screamed the entire time," Fiona teased, and I rolled my eyes but laughed as I shrugged my shoulders, looking around the room. These things happened. When I caught her eye, Hailee smiled hesitantly at me.

"There's no time to waste. While my beautiful wife makes dinner, I'll take you guys out on the boat," Mr. Perez said. He clapped his hands twice and everyone stood. I opened my bag and pulled out my sunglasses. I had to ride in style of course. The walk down the path to the dock was silent, but the excitement was palpable. When we got to the SS *Perez*, we stood in a single-file line to have sunscreen sprayed on us while Mr. Perez told embarrassing childhood stories about the person getting the sunscreen. Charlie's story was about the time she fell face first into dog poop; Fiona farted really loudly in a very quiet room and sat in peanut butter. My story probably wasn't going to be as bad compared to Olivia's—she'd had to walk around the park all day with red paint on her dress, because she'd thought wiping her hands on her dress would get the paint off of her fingers. Mr. Perez told the story about Hailee eating lipstick because she thought that was how you got it on your lips. I was last to get sprayed because I needed help getting in the boat.

To close out, Mr. Perez recounted the time they all found me on the ground eating bugs, worms, and mud because one of the boys up the street, Jackson Hines, told me it would help me grow. In my defense, I'd hated being the shortest in the group even then. Once I was safely in the boat, I moved to the built-in benches at the front. I leaned back, crossing one leg over the other, and pulling down my sunglasses to the tip of my nose like I'd seen too many times in movies. I waved at Fiona who was across from me on the other bench and turned back toward the water as Mr. Perez started the engine and pulled away from the dock.

I loved being on the boat. I loved the feeling of the wind in my hair and the smell of the lake filling my nose as we moved further out. I pulled my phone out of my pocket to take pictures.

"Love you!" I texted the group chat and smiled at every response calling me a sap. In truth, I always got extra emotional on the water. Maybe it was the way I always felt renewed the moment my body entered the water; all the possibility I saw in that. As much as I loved my everyday life, I loved the fact that our summer weekend lake house trips made me feel like the world was smaller, in a way that calmed me, the very moment I needed it most. When the boat came to a stop, I smiled and sat up on the bench. The sun shone down on me and I looked over at Fiona, who was already pulling her oversized shirt off so she could get in. I joined her and slid off my jean shorts and tank top. We went to the back of the boat to find Olivia, Hailee, and Charlie already swimming.

"Come on, Fi and Drea. Water feels great," Charlie announced before plugging her nose and going under. Olivia swam over to help me in. Fiona held the top of the ladder as I climbed down. On the last rung, Olivia took my free hand so I wouldn't lose my balance when I let go with the dominant one.

When we were all in the water, we swam to the front of the boat and let ourselves float and relax, splashing each other and laughing as Mr. Perez sang the songs on the radio loud enough for us all to hear.

~~~

When we got back inside the house, we all crashed on the couch. Charlie turned on the TV and we watched something about a person who faked their death and was now out for revenge. I was absolutely invested in "helping" this woman find justice. Me and Patricia were well on our way to catching her husband red-handed for framing her son—I knew I couldn't trust him because he didn't have kind eyes. We'd found the secret passport and life insurance policies she never knew about, but halfway through, Mr. Perez came into the living room, cutting our journey short. Godspeed, Patricia.

"Take the bags upstairs, ladies. After you wash your hands, we can eat!" Mr. Perez said. His curly black hair fell in his face the way Charlie's did when she forgot to tie it back. I smiled at their dad and grabbed my bag.

"Wait, usual arrangement?" Charlie asked, grabbing her bag and heading toward the steps. She looked back when she reached the bottom. Olivia, Hailee, and I stood up at the exact same time, ready to go upstairs. Fiona was the only one who lagged, texting on her phone.

"Works for me," Hailee said, looking at me. Sleeping in the same room would be fine; we used to do it all the time, right? Right. Everything was going back to normal, just the way I wanted, except now I was wary of it. Why was everything going back to normal now? We really went at each other and haven't talked about it yet . . . why? My heart was racing like it did at the start of a roller coaster. Hailee was waiting for me to agree, and all I could hear was my hammering heart. No, this was fine, it was going to be fine.

To my credit, I tried to appear as nonchalant as possible, making a noncommittal noise of agreement instead of answering outright. My focus went to adjusting the strap on my bag as I moved toward the steps. Charlie climbed them with ease. I grabbed the railing and made my way up, knowing it was not going to be that easy—it almost never was. I was aware that both Olivia and Hailee were behind me, which made me trip up trying to go faster than I should've. I hated the way my bag slapped against my leg as I moved, but I needed to carry it myself. When I reached the top, I sighed in a small relief. Making my way to the door on the right at the end of the hall was easy. As I set my bag down, Olivia popped her head in.

"Jamie just asked me to be his girlfriend!" she said excitedly. I squealed and pulled her into the room with a hug. The others joined us seconds later, each grabbing on to Olivia as she relayed the news, and by the end of it winding up in a pile on the floor.

"When did he ask? Tell us everything," Charlie said, her leg wrapped over Olivia, whose head was in Fiona's lap. Hailee's foot was hooked around mine, while my head was on

Charlie's stomach. I had no idea how we found these positions on the ground, but they were comfortable. As Olivia launched into the story, we all got to watch her face light up. She really deserved to be as happy as she was in this moment. We'd be having a Sunday dinner together again soon, for the first time in too many years, and I was really looking forward to it. As the story progressed, everyone began adjusting the positions they were in. Somehow, I ended up closest to Hailee, the butterflies I'd exiled returning with the confidence of a Disney movie villain. Still, I tried my best to focus on the story at hand because that was what Olivia deserved.

When we were done and everyone had taken their bags and gone to their separate rooms, Hailee and I remained. It was understood that I would take the bottom bunk while Hailee was fine to climb. Hailee walked over and set her bag down closer to the dresser. I watched her put her purse down too and pull her clothes out of her bag to put them away. She always was the first to unpack; she said it made her breathe a little easier. When she was finished, she sat next to me on the bottom bunk and exhaled deeply. She turned to me, nervous—like I wasn't too and hadn't already been looking at her. Then she got up and closed the door before returning to the bed, her eyes back on me. It was rare, but I couldn't tell what she was thinking, or what she might say as our breaths mixed together in the otherwise empty space.

"You're right next to me and I still miss you," Hailee said simply. She looked away from me.

I sat there stunned. She missed me. Me. All this time, I'd thought I'd been the only one missing her, wanting everything to go back to the way it was. I'd thought Hailee was so upset and angry that she didn't want to be friends. Knowing that I wasn't alone in this made me want to do an end zone dance, or do backflips down the hall.

Hailee looked back at me like she might cry, though there was only an inch between us. I couldn't have Hailee crying again, not because of me. I grabbed her hand and kissed it in apology, shocking us both. Weird as it was, I found that I didn't regret it. Instead, I looked Hailee in the eyes as I lifted my head from her hand. I squeezed it and then let it go.

"I miss you all the time, Hails. I really messed things up for us, I know. We haven't had time to talk without arguing and I—" She cut me off by pressing a finger to my lips. I looked at her, confused. Why was she stopping me in the middle of my apology? We couldn't get past this if we didn't talk. "Hailee, come on we need to—" And then she leaned over and kissed me. I almost fell back at the contact, but Hailee grabbed my arm to keep me in place.

SHE KISSED ME. AGAIN.

I was too surprised to kiss her back, worried she'd just regret it again—regret *me* again. That is, until Hailee began pulling away. I chased after her lips with my own, deepening the kiss as I went. Hailee's lips were as soft as I remembered, and I could taste the cherry lip gloss that I used to watch her reapply in between classes at school. I pulled her bottom lip into my mouth and was pleased to find that, unlike weeks before, Hailee didn't pull away this time: she leaned into it. Our tongues found each other's and I couldn't hide the small noises escaping my mouth; I was grateful I didn't have to. Hailee laid me back and I lost myself under the weight of her. We stayed like that for only a moment, but I could've stayed there forever, kissing and pulling each other close. I needed air to breathe, though, unfortunately, so I pulled away first, smiling as Hailee blushed. She kissed me quickly a few more times just to make sure we weren't dreaming.

"That was an interesting turn of events," I said, letting Hailee take my hands and kiss the backs of both. We giggled at the action. At least I didn't have to feel silly about doing it earlier. Hailee was looking at me like she'd just won the lottery. I couldn't wait to do it again. Why wait? I was gearing up to lean in once more when Hailee's face turned serious.

"Drea, the real reason I was upset about you and George was because . . . I wanted it to be me. You and I have history, but I was so scared that you'd break my heart. I was scared I wouldn't be enough for you; I mean, you thought I didn't even like girls. The only reason I said the kiss was a mistake was because I didn't know if you were just kissing me back to make me feel better. I didn't want a pity kiss; I wanted the real thing. And then I came over, and he kissed your cheek, and I knew I'd lost you," she said.

I moved to respond, to tell her that she hadn't lost me at all. In fact, I wanted her to know that she never would—but Hailee stopped me.

"Let me get this out please. You dating George didn't make me realize I am in love with you. I realized it at the first school dance this year, when we were dancing under the lights. When you laid your head on my shoulder? I was afraid to breathe—it felt like we were the only ones in the room. You are one of the most beautiful people in the world and I—"

"I want to kiss you so bad," I interrupted, and so we kissed and kissed. When we pulled apart, Hailee swatted my hand.

"You're interrupting my speech. I practiced and everything," she complained. I interlocked our fingers and pouted in mock apology.

"Sorry, go ahead," I said.

"You are one of the most beautiful people in the world and I am glad you are starting to see what everyone else has already seen. And I don't want houses next door, I want a big bed with an en suite bathroom and your clawfoot tub. I'm sorry I took so long to tell you how I feel and I really want to kiss you again, now that I'm done," Hailee finished. She bounced up and down on the bed and grabbed my hands.

"So, we're both sorry, and we both really want to keep kissing each other?" I asked, and Hailee nodded eagerly, closing her eyes and puckering her lips. I laughed and let go of her hands and stood. I needed to stretch after sitting for the majority of the day. Hailee joined me moments later and began to stretch too. Left-toe touches to right-toe touches and lunges for good measure. After we collectively completed them, Hailee turned to me, her hand outstretched and eager.

"Also, now that you know I like you and you like me, I think we should date." She kissed my hand and giggled before looking back up at me, her eyes hopeful.

I smiled and got down on one knee. Laughing, I grabbed Hailee's hand. "Will you be my girlfriend, Hailee Tsang?"

"Yes! Now I get to kiss you whenever I want," she laughed, helping me up. We hugged before we sat back down and she looked at me seriously.

"I hope you know that I think you are funny, gorgeous, talented, and anyone would be lucky to call you their girlfriend. I'm going to shout it from the rooftops if you let me. I mean that." I couldn't find the words to express all of the gratitude, relief, excitement and joy I was feeling, so I did what any smart teenage girl my age would do. I kissed her instead.

We stayed in our little bubble for a little while longer before we were pulled back to reality as knocks sounded on the door.

"You told her?" Olivia squealed. She hopped in place where she stood and Fiona fist-bumped the air. We were smiling just as hard at our friends' approval. Fiona squeezed my side and asked us if we'd thought about couples' costumes for Halloween. Olivia reminded her that it was a little early for that, and she countered that it was never too early to start planning.

"Genuinely happy for you both," Charlie said, smiling as she made her way to the downstairs. Hailee held my hand until we got to the first step, letting go so I could hold onto the railing. When we reached the bottom, our hands found each other's again. As we ate dinner, I thought about the new adventure we were headed on and how excited I was about it. This time, when our legs touched under the table, I didn't jump out of my chair. I didn't have to—I simply turned to my girlfriend and winked, and took another bite of pulled pork.

Later, we called and told our parents the good news. Janice cried tears of joy and my parents announced that they always saw Hailee as their daughter anyway, so now it would just be in-law. If I could blush, I would've at that moment. Hailee took it in stride, though, surprising us all with a little smile, "Someday."

~~~

"I love this song," Fiona shouted as she turned up the stereo in the living room. The song changed and we busted out the dance routine we'd made up for the middle-school talent show. Olivia began in the center of the room, her hands on her hips, while Fiona and I stood to her sides, our hands on our right knees; Hailee and Charlie stood on either side of us, and when the beat dropped, we set in motion. I moved my hips to the left and the right with Olivia; Fiona and Charlie dropped it low; while Hailee's body rolled. We went through the rest of the routine like a well-oiled machine. For our closing poses, I ended up in the middle with my arms across my chest and Charlie in front of me, leaning on one knee; Fiona to the left of us, her hands on her hips; Olivia to the right in a split; and Hailee to the right of Olivia, one of her hips cocked to the side with a "tough girl" look on her face. When the song ended, we burst into laughter. We danced together happily for a few more songs. Hailee ran over to me and took my hands—she had to yell a little bit for me to hear her over the music. All of us were grateful that Mr. and Mrs. Perez were out on a date.

"It's no Blueberries, but it's . . ." Hailee began, licking her lips—and I'll admit I was distracted for a second.

"Perfect," I replied, smiling wide at her and then to the others. High on the sugar rush from eating a bunch of Dots, Olivia threw her fist in the air.

"Cross it off the list!" she shouted to a chorus of approval from Hailee, Fiona, and Charlie. I pulled out my phone and scrolled to the note.

## THE BSE (Best Summer Ever) LIST!

1. ~~Blueberries~~
2. ~~Art show in ShoeHorn~~
3. ~~Lizzo concert~~
4. ~~thrift shop pop-up~~

5. Skinny-dipping at the lake house
6. ~~Amusement Park Day!~~
7. Drew Barrymarathon
8. ~~Paintball Day~~

"It's off the list," I announced to another round of cheers. We turned down the music and changed into our pajamas before piling back onto the couch to watch as many movies as our eyes would allow. I spent the majority of the first two movies watching the sun fall and the water ripple. Hailee was curled into me, and she smelled like lavender. Every few minutes I could feel her eyes on me, and I wrapped my arm around her waist and smiled as Fiona laughed out loud at something happening on-screen. I turned back toward the TV and gave it my full attention. In the movie, the main character and the love interest readied themselves to jump in the lake to escape the people on motorbikes shooting at them. Hailee poked my side and smiled at me conspiratorially.

"I have an idea," she announced.

"I don't know if I like that look on your face, Hails," Olivia said. Fiona paused the TV and turned to give Hailee her full attention.

"I don't either," I agreed. Hailee pulled away from me to address the room, but kept her hand on my knee. She cleared her throat and tucked her hair behind her ear like she was gearing up to give a speech. We laughed at her extra-ness, but she pressed on.

"We should go skinny-dipping," Hailee said decidedly. She immediately looked at me. I raised an eyebrow at her. Fiona shot up from the couch, her hair falling out of her loose ponytail.

"Yes!" she said excitedly. I looked at Fiona, who just shrugged at me. I couldn't blame her; not really. I knew she'd be the first to agree. "Drea, you're always talking about making memories—this is the perfect one to make."

I looked to Olivia, who stood up to grab a bottle of water from the kitchen. We all watched her silently. When she sat back on the end of the couch furthest from Hailee and me, and took a swig of water, Fiona groaned in frustration. Olivia didn't even try to hide her laughter.

"You in, Liv?" Fiona finally asked, her eyes pleading. I was definitely going to lose this fight if Fiona was pulling out the puppy dog eyes. I suspected it wouldn't take much for Olivia to agree, though, given her whole "we'll only look like this once" philosophy.

"It *is* on the list, Drea," Olivia turned to me with a smile. I was outnumbered. Just then, Charlie bounced back down the stairs from the bathroom. "You in Char?" Olivia called out to her.

"Yes," Charlie said easily. I didn't even hide my scoff.

"You don't even know what you just said yes to!" I cried, looking around for the support I knew I wouldn't find.

"Doesn't matter. If we're all doing it together, I'm in," Charlie decided, walking over to link arms with her sister. Hailee squeezed my knee and looked back at me. My heart began to race. I knew I wasn't going to say no to her.

"Baby—" Hailee sighed, grabbing my chin and kissing me.

"She's definitely in," Charlie teased. I pulled away from Hailee to throw a pillow at her, and she dodged the first but wasn't quick enough to miss the second. Fiona laughed but threw one back at me. She had to defend her sister; it was code or something apparently. I stood and ran a hand through my hair. Fiona left a note for her parents just in case they came back before us.

> *Out swimming near the dock. We'll stay in sight of the house.*
> *Love you,*
> *The Breakfast Club*

"Let's go," I said, the smile spreading across my face genuine. Hailee grabbed my hand and Olivia grabbed hers; Charlie was next and Fiona on the tail end. We ran to the dock like it was a race. We peeled our clothes off quickly and jumped in.

The water was freezing, our mingled laughter the only thing keeping us warm. It looked almost black from where we floated. The only light came from the row of phones we'd left on the dock with the flashlight function on, so we could see a little bit. Olivia was the first to splash me, swimming away before I could get my revenge. I tried to hold my breath underwater with Fiona, and waded around with Charlie chatting. It really was the perfect night. One I would never forget.

"Fancy meeting you here," Hailee said softly, as I turned around to face her. Our matching smiles made my heart race. She swam closer—we were only an inch away from each other. I could feel her body heat. "You are so gorgeous."

I closed the distance between us, wrapping my arms around her neck. I was keenly aware of the fact that our bodies were touching, but I didn't linger on it. We swayed to a song in our heads; I looked past her and watched the trees sway too in the wind. When I looked back, Hailee was leaning in for a kiss. I pulled back. She whined, but didn't let me go.

"You know, I've been thinking. I should get a reward for doing this," I started, smiling as I leaned further back. I was still close, just not close enough to kiss.

"I'm trying to reward you right now," Hailee said. She leaned closer, but I kept ducking her. She huffed. She was so cute poking out her bottom lip because she wasn't getting her way.

"I want to negotiate," I replied, nodding my head firmly like this was a business deal.

"I'm listening." This time, when she leaned in, so did I.

"I want to pick our first date spot," I said excitedly. Hailee spun us around in a circle.

"Deal," she answered easily.

"Really?" I asked, the happiness in my voice clear.

"Yes, I had a whole thing planned, but this works too. Now come here," Hailee demanded, and I did. We kissed slowly, my arms laid around her neck, and the world fell away. That is, until Olivia, Fiona, and Charlie began splashing us. Then we had to separate to defend ourselves. Fiona was the first to raise the white flag.

"I'm getting pruned. Can we go in?" she asked, already making her way to the dock. We all followed in silent agreement. After we dried off, got dressed, and went back inside, we finished the movie. Everyone felt a little gross, so we took turns showering and said goodnight to Charlie and Fiona's parents when they came back. I slept the best I had in weeks.

~~~

Now that Hailee was officially my girlfriend, we were kind of both obsessed with the word. We didn't hammer on the PDA at the house, because we weren't that insufferable, but we often referred to each other by the title and not our names. This earned quite a few eye rolls, but it was worth it.

@HaileeTxo: Look at how cute my GIRLFRIEND is?

Hailee posted, attaching a picture of me with my legs up on the bench looking out at the water. What the picture didn't show was that shortly after, Olivia almost dropped her phone in the water after she'd snatched it back from Fiona, who had asked her four questions that she was too engrossed to answer. Fiona decided she'd had enough of Olivia being on her phone talking to Jamie, so she started playing hot potato with Charlie—the phone as the potato. Once Olivia's phone was safe and sound, we made a pact to just be with each other when we were with each other. Sure, Hailee and I had found a loophole around that, but we wouldn't abuse it.

Hailee, who was now fast asleep on my shoulder in the back of the car on the way home, made me feel like this new addition to our relationship was our best idea yet. Despite the fact that we would fall asleep on each other's shoulders before, this kind of thing felt different now—it *was* different. My stomach had more butterflies in it than a conservatory and now that Hailee and I were dating, I could let them stay awhile. I could count the freckles on her face and be rewarded with a kiss on the cheek. So far, the whole relationship thing was pretty great.

"Earth to Drea," Olivia said, from the other side of me. Olivia waved her hand in my face for good measure, effectively knocking me out of my own thoughts.

"Sorry, Liv. What's up?" I asked, taking a second to look at my friend. Olivia's hair was tied in a loose bun on the top of her head. She placed her sunglasses on her forehead and raised an eyebrow at me.

"If we hadn't all been waiting for this for ages, this would be annoying," Olivia said, gesturing between Hailee and me. I rolled my eyes but kept the smile on my lips. I tried my best to wink at her, but both my eyes closed, which made us laugh. "Your Mom asked if chicken penne pasta was good enough for dinner?" Olivia asked.

"Yes! But why didn't she just text me?" I looked at my phone though I knew I hadn't missed a call. Olivia shrugged and sang along to the song on the radio, then turned back to me.

"Oh, because we were already talking about Fashion Week. I'm sorry if I was overstepping, but I just said I'd ask since I was right next to you," she said, her direct eye contact and the pitch change in her voice making me regret the question. I rushed to reassure her.

"It's fine, Liv. Seriously. Just don't be surprised when Daddy asks Jamie over for one of his 'talks,'" I added, putting air quotes around the last word. I watched and laughed as Olivia placed her head in her hands in mock horror.

"It's going to be the worst, and I can't wait," she said easily. Charlie and Fiona began singing a Spanish song that I didn't know, but I tapped my foot along to it anyway.

"So, when is D Williams going to have that talk with Sleeping Beauty over here?" Olivia gestured to Hailee, who was now absolutely beginning to drool. It was actually cute.

"We were talking about it last night and we think that he already did. Remember when Hailee jokingly asked me to the school dance? The Sunday dinner before, he pulled her aside, and Hailee said he went on and on about loving us both, but needing to make sure that we were being safe and taking care of each other and our boundaries. Hailee couldn't leave until she promised to treat me right and take things slowly," I said. We both cringed and found ourselves laughing again.

When Mrs. Perez pulled into the driveway and turned off the engine, Olivia was the first to hug her, Mr. Perez, Charlie, and Fiona before exiting the SUV. She grabbed her bag and mine from the trunk and walked toward the door. Hailee and I said our goodbyes to everyone with hugs and air kisses, as was tradition. We watched the SUV peel off, and Hailee slung her bag over her right shoulder so she could hold my hand with her left. We walked inside for the first time as girlfriends, took off our shoes, and were greeted by Janice, my parents, Liv, Merv, and Andrew, who were already sitting at the dinner table, clapping like the pilot had just safely landed the plane. We leaned into it, bowing dramatically before walking over to the other side of the table where two empty seats were waiting for us.

~~~

"And then, Olivia fell face first into her mud pie," Andrew said, closing off a climax to a really funny story.

"Good one, MJ," I said, reaching across the table to high-five him. A high five he mock sighed and accepted. Olivia groaned and looked to Janice for help—she was always good at changing the subject. Janice, to her credit, did just that. She gave everyone an update on her new jewelry that she was finally ready to sell online, and she reiterated her support of Hailee's and my new relationship with an "I told you so" to everyone at the table, including the two of us. I loved Mama J so much. Once dinner was done, Dad went in the kitchen to get the dessert. The smile that formed on my face when I saw the apple pie and vanilla ice cream was wide and eager. My phone dinged in my pocket, and I pulled it out to find a text.

Hails: Why are you so cute though? ❤

Andrea: Good genetics and humility

Hails: Yeah, that must be it ☺

Andrea: You're cuter ❤

"Put your phones down and eat your dessert," Dad chided. Hailee and I did as we were told, stealing glances and smiles at every moment we could while the conversation happily buzzed around us.

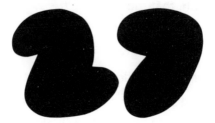

The summer days flew by, Hailee and I spent the time kissing in between customer visits at work, Olivia became a regular at Sunday dinners again, and before we knew it, August 1st was here. I was both grateful for that and nervous as Mom put the finishing touches on my outfit. A little piece of everyone was with me today, whether it was the purple bracelet as a nod to Hailee, the black earrings for Uncle D and Fredrick, the black low-heeled boots for me, or the colored patch dress I wore, hoping it squeezed in everyone I loved as well as my portrait did.

"Wearable art for the artist," Mom said when she was done fussing over me. I would never say it aloud because it was such a cliché, but as we climbed in the car to go and set my portrait up early, I felt like I'd already won.

Each young emerging artist had been given a time slot to set their work up in their designated area. I chose the time slot closest to the start of the showcase so my nervous energy had a distraction. This year, we weren't in a gallery, but I liked the new setup much better. The showcase was in a warehouse with high ceilings and lots of pendant lighting, and though the bones were very gray and concrete-focused, the plethora of colorful art that covered the warehouse was a great offset. The other artists were around me, bustling and busy. They wanted this just as bad as I did.

Last year, I had gone in thinking that I was going to lose. I was defeated before I stepped foot inside, so certain that the judges would take one look at my landscape and feel uninspired—and they had. This year was my last chance—I'd be eighteen before next year's deadline—and this time I felt like I actually had one. I stopped to chat with Victor, an artist I'd met at my first ever showcase two years ago.

"You look great," Victor said, hugging me quickly. I beamed at him and pointed to the curl on the front of his head.

"Okay curl, who are we trying to impress? You look handsome," I said. Victor leaned forward so I could see it better.

"This old thing?" Victor shrugged, winking. I could hear the laughter in his voice. Tonight, he wore dark jeans cuffed at the ankle, a white T-shirt, and a leather jacket. He looked very much like James Dean. I looked past him to find his self-portrait. He'd painted the trans flag in the background behind his smiling face in a motorcycle jacket, jeans, and sunglasses. So, he was a companion piece to his art as well—great minds think alike. He'd painted himself leaning against a tree.

"Charlie is coming tonight," I teased, laughing at the blush and slight panic that rose on his face. Charlie and Victor met during an ice cream run at a sleepover last school year. I'd seen him just after we ordered and immediately ran over for a hug. As we all waited for our orders, I caught a front-row seat to see them hitting it off. After giving Charlie the nod of approval, they'd exchanged numbers before we left to go back to the house. I had no idea if they kept in touch, but, judging from the look on Victor's face, the spark was still there.

"Cool, that's really cool. I love your portrait by the way—you look great!" Victor said, eager to change the subject. Still, I noted that he checked himself out when he pulled his phone out of his pocket. By the time my parents made their way back toward us, I had already wished Victor luck and promised to let Charlie know that he was here too. We walked back over to my painting and I snapped a picture for Vanessa and Faye.

> Fayelala: I know that we see you in like two week-
>      ends but I'm sad we couldn't be there tonight to
>      see it in person
> Nessa: Just kidding, we're here! look up!!

I glanced up and across the way, and there Faye and Vanessa were. We let out a joint squeal and met each other in the middle.

"What are you two doing here? I thought you had rehearsal, Faye . . . and you told me you had a family thing, Nessa!" I chided, smiling from ear to ear.

"That's how surprises work, silly!" Vanessa teased, slapping her own knee like a dad with a really corny joke.

"I love you both so much!" I squealed again, jumping up and down in my spot a little. "I can't believe you're here!"

"We love you too, go knock them dead," Faye added, kissing my cheek. "Also, looks like someone has been waiting to talk to you," she whispered with a smile, nodding her head to behind me as she and Nessa left to explore the space. I turned around to find the culprit walking over.

"Hi," Hailee said.

"Hi," I repeated, taking her hands. We stood like that for a few moments until a throat cleared. We turned to find that the throat belonged to Fiona, who giggled immediately afterward. I let Hailee go and moved to hug both Fiona and Charlie, who blushed after I told her Victor was here. Charlie made her way over to him, pulling Fiona along for moral support. Mr. Perez and Mrs. Perez came in shortly after with Olivia. Mr. Perez and Mrs. Perez hugged me first, with encouraging words about how talented I was, then turned to make conversation with my parents and Mama Janice.

Olivia hugged me next and I found that we had in fact gotten better at the hugging aspect of our rediscovered genuine friendship. Olivia walked over to join Fiona and Charlie. I was still stuck on the fact that everyone was there to support me tonight—Faye and Vanessa had made it, Uncle D, and Fredrick in spirit—and I felt them every time I looked at my self-portrait.

I knew that it was now time for the judges to start to circle and ask each artist about their entry. I smiled brightly as they walked up to me. The first judge, Lewis, was an older Black man with the bone structure of a former model; he had his salt-and-pepper hair pulled back into a ponytail to be kept out of his face. His resting face was serious, but I could see the light behind his eyes. A well-decorated artist in his own right, he was most known for his mixed-media art, but his talent made it clear that he could probably create whatever he wanted to and have it end up a masterpiece.

The other two judges this year were new to the show-case, but I had done my research. Anna was a murals artist whose stuff I had drooled over online. She was a white woman with short brown hair and sleeves of tattoos; she smiled gently at me. The final judge was my actual hero: Alexis Sher-wood, a Black woman in her mid thirties with long black hair and a birthmark on her left cheek. She specialized in street art, nature, and human portraits. I still couldn't believe it. Alexis Sherwood was looking at my work. We were mere inches away from each other. Before I could even think, it was like my mouth began moving on its own.

"I love you," I said, immediately clamping my hand over my mouth. "Oh my gosh, I'm so sorry," I said just as quickly. I looked over at my parents, who mouthed at me to breathe. So, I took a quick inhale and turned back to the judges. They were all now smiling at me.

"Tell us about your work tonight," Alexis said. She stood with her hands clasped in front of her, and all I could think about was that these were the legendary hands that made my favorite art: her abstract portraits using oil paints, watercolor, and acrylics. I thought of my favorite recent collections of hers, where she had painted people and made some of their facial features different types of flowers. It was so cool. I sighed, overwhelmed with excitement, then remembered that I was supposed to be speaking.

"My self-portrait is titled: *I am who they make me.* I was struggling to complete this piece for the showcase for a while. I'm seventeen and still figuring out who I can be, and I felt like there was pressure to figure out exactly who that person is. When my mother helped me realize that I didn't need all the answers right now, I titled it this way—because as much as we are our own people, I realized that the missing piece was the inclusion of the people who help make me the person that I am." I turned back toward the painting as I finished and stepped aside a fraction, so the judges could look at it closely.

"Great work," Anna said. I thanked her.

"I can see how proud you are of the people in your life, but more importantly, yourself. The technique here is wonderful," Alexis said.

"Thank you so much, Alexis Sherwood," I squealed out, closing my eyes in embarrassment. When I opened them, I was relieved to find that Alexis was laughing. I watched her look to her fellow judges like she was charmed by me or something. I was speechless.

"Alexis is fine," she replied. I smiled as she touched my arm briefly, grateful that she couldn't hear my racing heart.

"We have two more people to judge, but you've improved so much from last year," Lewis said. With one last nod, the judges moved on, and my friends and family rushed back over to congratulate me. Hailee handed me a plate of food and I ate it in the chair provided for me by Mr. Perez, while everyone talked amongst themselves.

As we waited, we made polite conversation with the guests around us and walked around a bit to see more of the art. Then I heard the chatter around me rise. The judges came back out. Alexis Sherwood held the prize envelope—I knew from past years that this contained a gift certificate to the art store in town. Anna held the modestly sized trophy. The room grew quiet as they walked back in. I set the plate aside so no one would step on it, and stood. My mom held one hand while Hailee held the other, but I could feel all of my people behind me.

"Tonight, all of you have showcased talent and heart well beyond your years, and though there can only be one winner, you should all be so proud of yourselves and each other. Please know that the decision was not easy, and that is a testament to the work here today," Lewis said. Anna and Alexis nodded their heads vigorously in agreement. Alexis cleared her throat and stepped forward.

"The winner of the Young Artist Showcase is . . ."

I felt like I was in the water again, rocking back and forth slowly with the waves while my hands were being squeezed. I felt my dad's hand on my shoulder as I took another calming breath. I stole a look at Victor, who was standing with his older brother, just as nervous as I was. I closed my eyes and reopened them. This summer really was far from over, and after everything that had happened, I was so ready to take it on. No longer did I think that I had to bide my time, waiting for my life to start—it had already begun, and it was my job to create something meaningful with it. I went through a lot this summer: a heartbreak, a friend breakup, two friend makeups, defending myself against cowards, a solo trip with my mom, cooking with my dad, and my first love. This summer threw many things at me that I wasn't expecting, but I was better for them now. A list was not the determining factor of my life— not anymore. What I'd found on the other side was so much more meaningful and exciting anyway. We'd finish the list, because we were already so close, but there was still more adventure out there for me to find. I couldn't wait.

"Andrea Williams!" Alexis Sherwood said, but I couldn't move. I was worried I misheard her, until my friends and family started jumping up and down around me, cheering me on.

"You did it!" Dad said, pulling me into a quick hug before pushing me toward the judges. I walked as fast as I could toward them and tried to find the words.

"I won," I said, still simply trying to process the news myself. I took the envelope held out of Alexis Sherwood's—I mean Alexis's—hand, and was surprised when she hugged me.

"You sure did. Keep going, you hear me? You've got something special," she whispered in my ear. I began to cry tears of joy, and after hours of keeping my emotions at bay, I let them go like floodgates. I wiped my eyes with my right hand and shook Lewis's and Anna's hand with my left. Dad ran up to grab the trophy for me as I began walking toward Victor. I wiped my eyes once more and handed him the envelope.

"This isn't a charity thing before you start. I just got new paints and I know you said you needed some, so take this. Even though I still won," I whispered, with a wink. Victor scoffed playfully, but hugged me back.

"I am happy for you, Drea," he said into my ear, squeezing me. "Go celebrate with your fam, and thank you."

I nodded my head and walked back over to my portrait. I couldn't stop looking at it in amazement. I won! Hailee came up beside me and bumped my shoulder. I turned to face her and stepped into her arms.

"So proud of you, A," she said, just before kissing me. I tasted the blueberry in her lip gloss and smiled. Hailee pulled away to spin me like she had months ago at the school dance. I couldn't stop the laughter that escaped my mouth. I felt like I was floating on air. "And it's not over yet—we still have two and a half weeks left. How do you feel?"

Tonight, we'd watch Drew Barrymore movies after celebratory ice cream at work, where Victor was hopefully going to ask Charlie out. I caught sight of them making heart eyes at each other while Fiona looked like the most supportive and proud sister in the world; I knew it wouldn't be long. My parents were busy beaming at me, standing next to Janice, Faye, and Vanessa, who all looked just as happy. I beamed back at them. I turned to find Olivia, who gave me a thumbs-up as she mouthed, *Love you.* I mouthed it back and turned toward Hailee's beautiful, waiting eyes.

"How do I feel?" I replied. "Best summer ever."

# ACKNOWLEDGEMENTS

My first thanks goes to Levine Querido for giving TSSP a loving home. To my editor, Nick Thomas! We did it, thank you thank you for everything! To my copyeditor, cover designer (Jade Broomfield) and illustrator (Vivian Lopez Rowe), your work does not go unappreciated. Thank you!

To my literary agent, Alex Slater: ANOTHER ONE! Thank you for rocking with me. Only up from here!

To my best friends, you know who you are, I love you. So many of these moments—the support, guidance, and joy—were modeled after moments we have shared over the years. Every singing-in-the-car moment, specifically. This book is only possible because I had your love first. Thank you for letting me sing so loudly and so off-key. Thank you for being!

To my family, thank you for your endless support! I hope I make you proud. To my mommy, Evelyn Williams is only a fraction as cool as you!

Roxane Gay, my very own Alexis Sherwood, thank you for seeing me. I can't believe I get to be friends with someone as cool as you. Meeting your heroes rules!

Jennifer Pooley, my fellow lover of love stories and rom coms! Thank you for your constant encouragement and everlasting belief in me. Adore you!

Selma Blair, AKA my favorite Mean Baby, many of the moments of anniversary party magic, comfort, and softness were pieces of magical and real moments I was lucky enough to have with you. Thank you for your friendship and your humor. Let's celebrate this in a fancy hotel somewhere soon. Love you, B. Always.

Troy Nankin, my partner in crime, The bops we love filled the playlist I wrote this book to. So you were with me every step of the way. I love you, I do!

Mandy Moore, AKA AMG, my Rom Com queen, grateful for your friendship. I know these characters would adore you as much as I do. I know for a fact, on the warmest of summer days, Andrea has "Extraordinary" playing on her phone. I do, too. Love you!

Drew Barrymore, I don't know if you will ever read these words, but your work and you mean the world to me. Thank you does not even suffice. Every main character I create is just hoping to be as charismatic, joyful, honest, and full as the characters you've given to us. I have had many Drew Barrymarathons in my lifetime and I will continue to. I hope we meet one day and I get to tell you in person.

And finally, to my readers, my queer community, the disability community, and my fellow hopeless romantics, I am a fan first. I wrote this for us because we deserve love too. I hope that this book allowed you to feel seen and understood, that you left these pages with hope for your own love stories. I'm leaving these pages with hope of my own. I love us.

# ABOUT THE AUTHOR

CARISSA KING PHOTOGRAPHY

**Keah Brown** is a journalist, screenwriter, and author of *The Pretty One* and *Sam's Super Seats*. She is the creator of #DisabledAndCute. Her other work has appeared in *Teen Vogue, Elle, Harper's Bazaar, Marie Claire UK*, and *The New York Times*, among other publications. She has been featured in anthologies including the *New York Times*-bestselling *You Are Your Best Thing* edited by Brené Brown and Tarana Burke.

To learn more check out keahbrown.com.

## SOME NOTES ON THIS BOOK'S PRODUCTION

The front cover was designed and illustrated by Vivian Lopez Rowe; art direction and design for the jacket, case, and interiors was done by Jade Broofield. The text was set by Westchester Publishing Services, in Danbury, CT, in Georgia, a typeface created in 1993 for Microsoft by British designer Matthew Carter, inspired by 19th century Scotch Romans designs; the name of this serif refers to a tabloid headline, "Alien heads found in Georgia." The display type and chapter headers were hand-lettered by Broomfield. The book was printed on 78 gsm Yunshidai Ivory uncoated woodfree FSC™-certified paper and bound in China.

Production supervised by Freesia Blizard<br>Editor: Nick Thomas<br>Assistant Editor: Irene Vázquez

LEVINE QUERIDO